DREAMS OF GLASS

VOLUME ONE

A Mystery

BY J.T. CECIL

To my devoted parents, Tom & Christina,
who have always been there for me,
and who equipped me to begin this endeavour.

And to my loving wife, Sophia,
who inspired me to finish it...

Last Reminiscence

Once upon a rainy morn' on the windy shores of England, a tall and slender navy-man hid his son farewell.

"Chin-up, little one." said he, as his boy clung fast his knee; "You needn't fear; your family's here." And tears began to swell.

"Will I never see you again, Papa?" sobbed the little one of four.

"Oh, keep me in your heart and do not forget me, and I will be with you forevermore." said the man, kneeling, with one hand on his little boy's little heart, and with the other, wiping away his little tears. "I will always love you, my son."

Then once after a long embrace the sad sojourner embarked.

And slowly, so ever slowly, the tall ship with her tall captain slipped away quietly, into the curtains of mist...

DREAMS OF GLASS

C O N T E N T S

1

STANDING BEFORE THE OCEAN

The old man sat back in his armchair, staring out his large pane window. His grey eyes were unmoving – fixed on the splendid city that glistened in the late afternoon sunlight – gazing at the jagged skyline that stretched from one horizon to the other. He was a well-dressed gentleman, pale in colour, clean-shaven and bald. The look on his face was a look of sadness and deep thought. I wondered if he knew the reason for my visit.

I sat quietly on the ottoman in front of him as he sipped his herbal tea. He extended his hand towards the tea tray on a little table, motioning to me to go ahead and serve myself. He may have been sickly and tired, but when he fixed his eyes on me for a second, I could see that he was still sharp as a razor. Nothing seemed to escape his notice, including the drop of tea on the ottoman that I'd spilled and had tried to hide with a handkerchief. – The manservant standing by the door cleared his throat.

The air we breathed was warm and dry. It smelled of pine, paper and ink. Beams of yellow sunlight filtered in through the dim halls. We were sitting in a vast room, a library with a high moulded ceiling looming over us, with hanging lamps, and large pane windows stretching from floor to ceiling, shrouded on both sides with heavy red drapes.

Tall display cases were stationed between each window. Some were filled with old thick books. Others had displays of exotic plants and insects. There were racks of glass tubes filled with coloured fluids, and shelves of jars filled with minerals – all labelled and arranged neatly. Another case displayed several contraptions of brass and steel. And in the far corner of the library, the faint glow of a round computer screen was the only visible piece of modern technology in the room.

Picture frames lined the walls with photographs of my host with influential people at historical places. There were paintings, sculptures, artefacts and detailed maps and charts.

One could really sense that there was a great deal of history contained in this place. – As well there should've been. – This was, after all, the house of Lord Sage.

I dreaded the task I was here to do. The silly spoon fell from my teacup and clanged loudly against the hardwood floor, breaking the silence. I grabbed it from the floor in a flash, trying not to let it bounce. – The manservant standing by the door again slowly cleared his throat.

"Well, Mr. Addha" said Lord Sage with a smirk, as he finished his tea and placed his cup on the little table and folded his hands on his lap, "What shall we talk about this evening?"

"My lord, you know I'm not really so clumsy, only extremely self-conscious." I said as I put down my teacup.

"Relax, young man," he said as he glanced over at the manservant by the door, "...nobody's perfect." His eyes slowly returned to me. "Now please... state your business. – What is the reason for this unexpected visit?"

I stood up and bowed my head slightly. "My lord, with respect, I must inform you that evidence has been collected against you, and you have been summoned to be questioned by a comimission of the imperial court tomorrow morning at 10 hours. You and a few others are being investigated for conspiracy to undermine the empire. I'm sure you understand the need for such... short notice."

There was an eternal silence. I handed him the summons, but he made no movement. He just stared – as if he were looking right through me. The manservant morphed from a passive doorman into an imposing guardian as he approached with a menacing face.

"It's alright, Sid." said Lord Sage quietly, as he motioned him to take the summons from me, "...We knew this would happen."

He looked down for a moment and then turned his face again to the window. Our meeting was over.

Leaving that room and walking through the halls – through the huge wooden doors that led outside, and down the weathered stone steps – I felt like such a traitor. The house of Sage had stood as a living monument to the generations that had shaped our world. And now I was helping to tear it down.

Outside, the driver held open the shiny black door to the motorcar. I stopped and turned around to look behind and up at that house with those ancient stone towers. My hands tingled as I saw the last golden rays of sunset lighting up one side, and dark storm clouds descending upon the other. 'Prophetic', I thought as I got in and the driver closed the door. – It was the end of an age.

~~~

We drove off in the motorcar, rolling smoothly on its wide roller-belt of rubber and steel, following a long stone-paved road. The grounds looked beautifully kept with shady trees and lush green grass that carpeted either side of the road. There were these large blue flightless birds with long fanned tails, standing tall with their heads up high, watching us with their big black eyes as we passed by.

A sort of mist was blowing in through the trees. The sky was growing darker with rainclouds, and distant flashes of lightning gave warning of the rain that was coming.

We turned off the road, onto a downward ramp. The motorcar speed-up effortlessly as we descended onto a wide, partially covered freeway with some fast-moving traffic below ground.

The man I had just summoned to receive judgment was perhaps the last living key to solving one of the greatest mysteries of our world — a mystery that shrouded the very beginning of our civilization.

He belonged to a small group called the *Founders* — hard working men and women of honour who had helped rebuild our world after we had lost our way, after the Great Extinction and the long dark times that followed called the Aeonian Rift.

Everything in our world — our laws, our systems, our cities, our very way of life — all came from knowledge that the Founders carried with them. And all this knowledge was brought from an ancient race called the Perfectors — a people (as the legend goes) as old as time.

And whether those people were the originators or simply the caretakers of that knowledge, nobody knows. Nor is it known what happened to them. What is known is that they achieved greatness beyond imagination, only to become suddenly and completely extinct.

Now, after so much time had passed, our society had come to resemble an abandoned child that had grown up without its parents and now, as an adult, had become obsessed with finding them. The disappearance of the Perfectors had motivated the most ambitious endeavours of research and exploration, and had inspired countless works of art, music and literature.

But I had long felt that there was more at stake than just our own frustrations with unanswered questions about their disappearance. It was a strange churning feeling in my gut. As if a shadowy monster from ancient history was lurking beneath the surface of current events. And I wasn't alone in this thinking: If we couldn't find out what happened to them, then we might be doomed to suffer the same fate – sudden and complete extinction.

And what troubled me the most was that there was overwhelming evidence that Lord Sage himself had destroyed a great deal of valuable knowledge, as well as property of the empire, including artefacts and other clues about the history of the Perfectors. – But how could that be?

The speeding car lunged up a ramp and onto a long bridge leading to a span across part of the bay. Treetops whizzed-by beneath us as the shiny black motorcar sped along the freeway, riding quietly on its roller-belt.

The capital, New Ryattii, came into view, like a gleaming mountain range under a cloudy evening sky. I looked over the notebook I'd prepared for the hearing the following day. It was quite dark now. Light flashed across the pages as streetlamps whizzed past my window. But I couldn't concentrate and put it away.

I wanted to do something. But I knew that as an agent of the

Empire, I was probably being watched. (In fact, though I hadn't realized it, there was another black motorcar following us with its lights turned off.) I was risking putting myself against the highest authority in the land. And the enforcer of that authority was notoriously unforgiving.

The pitter-patter of raindrops on the motorcar window captivated me as we made our way into the city. And I lost track of time.

Suddenly my eyes came into focus as we came down the Founders' Broadway. Towering monuments of stone and iron on either side were lit from beneath with an orange glow. They had been built to commemorate the Founders.

Their granite forms and faces, carved to almost fifty times larger than life, gazed down over the rainy Broadway. And, as we passed beneath them, an eerie feeling came over me. They seemed to be looking right at me, as if they were judging me.

A cold sweat came over me. I suddenly felt incredibly small as I realized I was contemplating a vast ocean of thousands of years of history. Little did I know that, willingly or not, I would have to cross that ocean – and risk losing everything.

– The Inevitable Quest
Interviews by Danae Southendorn

-PART 2-

Gwithian, England
Friday, April 25th, 1823

Smooth reflections of light and dark clouds danced and mingled on the surface of the sapphire sea. The evening sun emerged from beneath a cloud, sending orange strokes of colour that filled the air. And mist from the churning waves, rising near the shore, caught the brilliant beams of light.

Up a slope leading away from the sand, some children played with their dogs in a field of tall grass. The green and brown stalks swayed in unison, like waves in the wind. And a black-stone house perched like an owl atop the slope, overlooking the sea.

On the doorstep there sat quietly an older child, a boy with brown curly hair, looking intently out at the sea. And though the others would beckon him, he wasn't interested in playing so much.

The door behind him opened and a motherly person appeared. She called out to the little ones: "Come inside for dinner, if you please!"

But they feigned deafness, laughing, saying: "Sorry, mother, we can't hear you!"

She looked down and said to the older child: "David, would you please fetch the little ones?"

"Oh...Very well." he said, reluctantly, as he got up.

"I beg your pardon?" she replied with half a smile.

"Oh!" he said as his eyes met hers, "I mean, yes aunty."

Inside, a fatherly man with round glasses, had already seated himself at the table; and having just lit some candles, was now reading a book and making some notes. The little children came in, ran 'round furiously and finally sat down to eat, though still laughing. He closed the book and just looked at them in the eyes. And all of a sudden, they remembered their manners.

The older boy came in slowly after them and sat down. The family bowed their heads and quietly began eating.

"Are you all right, David?" asked his aunt in a soft voice. "You don't look all right."

There was a pause. "Yes, Aunty, I'm fine." David's grey eyes looked up at his cousins who sat across from him and beside him, and at Uncle John, all of them eating quietly. Then he looked down.

"Someone was looking for me in town today." said David, as everyone stopped eating and stared at him. "It was a strange old man. He said that my father had sent him. He said something about an inheritance." David looked at his aunt and then again at his uncle.

There was another pause. Uncle John put down his fork and knife. "Maybe you should start from the beginning, David."

And so, the boy began to relate his memory of the strange encounter...

〜〜〜

He had been working hard, off-loading boats and barges at the docks early that morning. After work, everyone gathered at the public house. A late breakfast was served, glasses were filled and singing and laughter filled the air. – Though, there was nothing inappropriate for a boy his age.

He was sitting on a stool by the bar, not really touching his food as he listened to Bill, the one-legged-bartender, laughing and talking of his adventure at sea, catching a great "100-foot" tuna. – insisting he had "a missing leg to prove it!"

It wasn't until the laughter stopped that the boy could hear the sound of rich leather boots walking confidently up to the bar from behind him. A reddish-brown cloak brushed his elbow. Two black gloves rested firmly on the bar top immediately beside his plate. He didn't look up. He had never seen gloves like these – fine leather, embroidered with gold.

"Excuse me, sir." said the stranger with an educated accent, though unfamiliar, spoken with authority, yet tempered with tact. "Are you the proprietor of this place?"

"Maybe." said bartender-Bill, blankly, as he dried a glass with a cloth.

"I'm looking for someone – a young man by the name of David Sage." he said as he looked around the room. "Is he here, by any chance?"

David cautiously looked up, wide-eyed, and then looked down again as the stranger turned back to the bar.

"Aye, he might be here about." said Bill, "Who wants to know?"

The stranger had a serious yet pleasant expression on his aged yet vibrant face. "Well," he said, "would you be so kind as to point him out?"

"Not sure I can." said Bill.

"Ah... Does not the proprietor of this place know his patrons when he sees them?" he asked with a chuckle.

"What do you take me for? Do I look stupid to ya?" retorted begrudged Bill. "I know everybody in this here town! – Everybody except *you*, that is!"

The stranger bowed his head slightly: "Forgive me, sir. I was not seriously implying any incompetence on your part. Nor do I wish any ill-will on your patrons. It is for a respectable business that I am here."

"Well, you do look respectable, I suppose, so... I guess I won't have you tossed out just yet."

"Thank you, sir." he said.

"What's this all about, then?" resumed Bill, with his nose pointed up in the air, "Is the boy in some sort 'a trouble?"

"If it was trouble I came for, I might resort to using force, would I not?" he said with a grin.

But Bill was not amused, and his eyebrows sank over his eyes: "What's this here business of yours that's so respectable that brings you way down here from..., err, where did you say you were from?"

"I am a friend of his father. It was he who sent me."

"HA!" burst Bill, slamming his hand on the bar top, "Now I *know* you're lying! His old man's been *dead* for *ten years*! – Died in the war, he did!"

David was staring up at the stranger in disbelief. And he saw this in the corner of his eye but pretended not to notice. "Of course." he answered, "You see, his father has left an inheritance for him."

"You're lying." said Bill.

"Am I?"

Bill then proceeded to bombard the fellow with words of a different colour.

Before anyone could take notice, David slipped out and ran down the road, and out of sight...

≈≈≈

"I got away from him without any trouble, uncle." said David, "He moves slowly and could not have followed me here, all the way from Hayle. He's probably just an old fool."

Uncle John took off his glasses and rubbed his eyes. He looked worryingly at his wife, then the children. Then he just gazed out the window from his chair for a minute.

"No, David..." he said, "He's no fool."

"What's wrong, Papa?" sobbed little Caleb as John got up from the table. "What's that bad man come for? Is he... is he come to hurt Dave? Oh, no! Is he come to take Dave away? Will we never see him again, Papa?"

David's eyes became unfocused as Caleb's tearful words rang

in his ears. They reminded him of something, and he became troubled. But he lost his thought.

"Never you mind." answered Caleb's mother, "Just finish your supper, please."

John took his coat and went outside and walked down to the sandy shore. Aunt Mary got up from the table, wrapped herself in a shawl, and ran out after him.

The sun was setting on the horizon and a soft breeze blew Mary's hair around wildly as she ran down the hill onto the flat sandy beach. She caught up to him, took his hand in hers, and they stood there quietly.

Golden beams of sunlight danced on the ocean waves. And the suds and salty water hissed and dabbled on the sand below their feet.

"I raised that boy as if he were my own son," said John, holding back tears. "...I promised his father I would protect him. I would've given him the world. And I would've done it for Hamilton, and for Isabel."

"It's our old friend again, isn't it?" said Mary "...That Mr. Grumman ...and after all this time!"

"Grumman!" John snickered as he shook his head. "That man took my sister's husband away. And now he's come for David."

"David's a smart lad." said Mary "You know he'll do what's expected of him. And he knows better than to take candy from strangers."

There was no answer from John, only a mournful sigh.

Mary continued: "I think he gets it from his uncle."

John smiled. "Oh, when did you get to be so wise?" he said lovingly, as he put his arm around her shoulder. But, as he was watching the setting sun, John's face sank into a deep sorrow. "I didn't want my sister to marry him, you know...

"It wasn't because of him... but... because of his *family*, especially his father. Oh, there was this *arrogance* about that man. Every word he spoke, every expression, every… everything… was so premeditated, so… weighed-out…

"Posh, I thought… It was as if he thought the whole world rested on his shoulders."

"Where are you going with this?" asked Mary.

"Well," continued John, "Looking back now, I don't think it really *was* arrogance I was seeing in him, but rather… the deepest sense of responsibility. And… I think Ham shared that sense too."

"Well, they both were British Navy-men." reasoned Mary.

"Yes, but I think it was more than that." said John, "I don't know what. But I think there must be something out there to account for it. And then there is this other matter of an 'inheritance'…" He paused for moment and sighed as he rubbed the back of his neck.

"I don't know." he continued, "Maybe they were scheming something or working on some diplomacy abroad. Or maybe they were on the verge of some great discovery. They were always talking behind closed doors, whispering in halls, and looking around to see if anyone was listening… It was as if they had some important part to play in something much bigger than you and me… grander than king and country… something so horribly marvellous we couldn't even imagine."

Mary was smiling at him. "Well… that's a relief!" she said, with a pause for suspense. "Well, our problems aren't as big as we thought then, are they?"

John laughed and kissed her forehead. He was stress-prone, and Mary always knew how to defuse a stressful moment. And he loved her for it. The sun now vanished behind the sea and the sky was dramatic in colour. Brilliant beams of gold, pink and red sunlight swept across the distant clouds as the sky grew dark.

And the wind let out one last restful sigh. "Oh! Just look at it, Mary!" marvelled John, "How small we are, standing before the ocean!"

2

SHADOWS OF
THE RAIN

The silence of the dark sleepy house was broken by the crackling spark of a match. A candle was lit. The match was blown out. A hand picked up the candleholder and the flickering light moved slowly down a narrow hallway. A door creaked open. Dim light entered, and two brown eyes surveilled the room. David was sound-asleep in bed, as were the two smaller boys in theirs. A book of poems lay open in David's hand, and an old-looking helmet sat on the floor next to his dusty shoes and some wooden toys. The light departed, and the creaky door closed.

The man in a robe, carrying the candle, continued slowly and quietly down the narrow hallway, past some little framed paintings of family ancestors. What was it that had so troubled David about those words little Caleb had spoken earlier at the table? That day had triggered such a flurry of unpleasant memories for everyone. But for David, it was his last reminiscence of his father that haunted him the most. – Not only because of what had happened, but because of what was said. His Uncle John recorded that moment for him in verse, which he would often read...

<<Once upon a rainy morn' on the windy shores of England, a tall and slender navy-man bid his son farewell.

"Chin-up, little one." said he, as his boy clung fast his knee; "You needn't fear; your family's here." And tears began to swell.

"Will I never see you again, Papa?" sobbed the little one of four.

"Oh, keep me in your heart and do not forget me, and I will be with you forevermore." said the man, kneeling, with one hand on his little boy's little heart, and with the other, wiping away his little tears. "I will always love you, my son."

Then once after a long embrace the sad sojourner embarked.

And slowly, so ever slowly, the tall ship with her tall captain slipped away quietly, into the curtains of mist...>>

Had David understood something hidden in those words? – A warning, perhaps? Did his father know he would not be returning? Or was David now seeing a connection? – Even suspecting that this strange new visitor had had something to do with the loss of his father? Might he now have realized that his own life might be in danger?

Fingers guarded the candle flame from the air as bare feet cautiously made their way down a dark staircase. The feet stopped precariously as a grey cat scurried down the stairs between them, almost causing an accident. Then the feet continued.

Dim candlelight now spread across the drawing room. Rain drops on a pane window reflected the candlelight as Uncle John came near.

He looked out into the rainy night and noticed a faint yellow light out in the bay. – A ship, perhaps? The cold glass window fogged over from his breath. He wiped it off and looked again. But the rain was picking-up and he couldn't see anything. – Did he just imagine it?

He was worried about David and didn't know what to believe. He rubbed the back of his neck as he turned around and looked at the little square clock with brass handles, ticking softly on the mantle, which read half-past midnight. And he started remembering some unsettling events of about ten years past.

It was in a great battle at sea, during the war of 1812, that David had lost his father. The little boy was only 4 years old at the time, and even then, it hadn't yet been a year since he'd already lost his mother in a tragic fire. So, at the time his father had become like an island to him, and a refuge. And so, he clung to him, as to a tree in a windy storm. But it was not to last. And though the boy didn't understand at first, it was made clearer to him as he grew.

The battle was intense. Out-gunned and out-maneuvered, with two enemy ships closing in on him, the young captain Hamilton Sage was doomed. Somewhere between the thundering cannons and the splintering masts, I was told, the unthinkable happened. And somewhere between the official letter of condolences and the formal farewell, a little boy's world came crashing down.

One by one, a hand began quietly taking old journals down from a dusty bookshelf and thumbing through them, by candlelight. Then the hand stopped. John held the candle closer.

Something had disturbed him about David's story. It was more than the obvious menace of an unwelcome visitor. No, it was something else, disturbing enough that he couldn't sleep at all. – Something he remembered reading about.

He began reading part of a page near the end of a journal, written by David's father about 11 years ago...

> <<...*The void in my heart has been unbearable. I can't stop thinking of Isabel. And I just can't stop thinking that my own brother might have had something to do with it. I mean, of all things - a fire!? - And by accident!? That house was the safest I'd ever known...*>>

John shook his head and looked away from the book, breathing heavily through his nose. His eyes fell on the candle beside him. And the flame, dancing at the top of the candle stick, captivated him as he remembered his sister's death. And he closed his eyes.

He skipped forward to the last few pages, written at a later date in that year...

> <<...*I have finally received it! –My commission as captain of the H.M.S. Phantom. We have one week to complete refitting the ship before departing on our mission. Perhaps this will bring some distraction from my sorrow, and a better life for my little boy when I return.*

My brother-in-law and his wife will take
care of little Dave in my absence...>>

He put down the book and double checked the others he had taken. There was something specific he was looking for. He reached up to the top shelf. There was an older, little book. He pulled it out and wiped off the dust. It was an earlier journal from much younger days. – Almost 20 years ago. Hamilton would've been a teenager when he wrote it.

John thumbed through it and stopped on a page with a symbol drawn on it; a large circle with a person in the middle, standing on the bottom edge of the circle; its head was wearing some sort of round hat at the centre of the circle; and its arms were outstretched and curved up to about the level of its head; and there were stars over its head.

In two lines around the edge of the circle were written words in a foreign language. There was no English written on that page, and no explanation on the surrounding pages.

John was puzzled. He was used to reading many books and considered himself to be well learned, at least, he thought, to be able to tell what language it was. But he couldn't. He'd never seen it before.

John turned back to an earlier page, which read...

<<...While the Phantom was waiting for
us, another ship, an old Turkish pirate ship
appeared out from behind St. Ives. They
were apparently startled to see a great
English frigate such as the Phantom
guarding the bay. And they swiftly turned
about and sailed off in a new direction.

We, however, were already rowing out in
a little boat, to join the Phantom. I was

rowing across the bay as hard as I could.
But they had already raised anchor and
were setting sail in pursuit of the pirates
that had just past so closely. And I had to
follow them for some time, rowing quite
some distance...>>

John's eyebrows squished together. He was unaware of this episode. He knew of rumours about Turkish pirates raiding nearby villages decades ago, but had never confirmed it, much less actually seen any himself. But this was not what he was looking for.

He turned about ten pages back to a slightly earlier entry – written a few days before that one. His eyes opened wide, and his lips quivered. This was it. He'd found what he was looking for. But he couldn't believe it, and he read it again slowly. It was an account eerily similar to what David had just described earlier that day. It read...

<<...It wasn't until the laughter stopped
that I could hear the sound of rich leather
boots walking confidently up to the bar
from behind me.
A reddish-brown cloak brushed my elbow.
Two black gloves rested firmly on the bar-
top immediately beside my plate. I didn't
look up. I had never seen gloves like these.
"Excuse me, sir." said the stranger with
an educated accent, though unfamiliar,
spoken with authority, yet tempered with
tact. "Are you the proprietor of this place?"
"Why? What do you want?" said Bill.
"I'm looking for someone; a young man by

the name of Hamilton Sage. I was a friend of his father's. And I bring his inheritance."
...>>

A sudden burst of wind and rain hit the window. John practically jumped out of his skin, shocked to the core.

He stood frozen for a second. He had dropped the book on the floor, and his hands trembled. He shook his head and snatched the book from the floor with a loud frustrated sigh, and shouted angrily towards the window, shaking his fist: "Why are you toying with us, Grumman?"

But, outside the window, his voice was lost in the rain and swallowed by the night.

～～～

Somewhere out there, in the darkness, after some time had passed, as the rain had tapered off, and the storm clouds had slowly parted, and the light of the full moon had spread over the sea, and the shadows of the clouds had drifted off, there came across the black waters of Corbis Bay a long rowboat with lanterns at the front and the back. Stealthily, it approached the docks near the town of Hayle as six oarsmen pulled quietly on their oars.

As they come alongside a dock the men held their oars straight up in the air, and when they were close enough, two others jumped onto it and tied the boat fast. Another man in a cloak got up and stepped out, while those who remained steadied the boat for him. He walked along the dock and into the town, carrying a glowing lantern with him.

At the edge of town, in the stillness of the night, a townsman awoke from his sleep to the rude sound of someone pounding on his front door. "Alright, alright!" he yelled, "I'm coming, I'm coming!"

Finally, he came and opened the door a crack. "Who is it?" he demanded.

"Excuse me, sir. Are you the blacksmith?" said a voice from under a cloak, standing out in the misty night.

"I might be. Why? What do you want?"

"I understand you might have a horse that I could borrow for a price."

He opened the door a little wider. "Well... I... uh..." but before he could answer, the stranger took a small sack full of gold coins and gave it to the man. "Well, uh, I mean, of course!" he stuttered, "Please..." he said, coughing a little after swallowing the wrong way. He slowly walked away from the door, clearing his throat. "Please... follow me."

-PART 2-

YEARS POST RIFT: 4142+516/516: RYATTII DIFFERENTIAL
LOWER CENTROID DISTRICT, NEW RYATTII

A long black table on a red carpet punctuated the dark conference room with glowing cool-white wall panels. Dozens of empty black chairs lined both sides of the table, each one with a silver table lamp in front of it.

But only one lamp was lit, near the far end. Beneath it laid a small open book with a hand skimming over it. I could hear the sound of whispering as the words were being read. Alone at the end of the table, sat a man engrossed in his lecture of what looked like an old journal.

"Excuse me, sir." I said cautiously, "The office is closed now.

Would you mind, you know, leaving... or something?"

Suddenly I felt the sharp pain of someone grabbing my arm. "Can we go now!?" asked an older sarcastic voice, spinning me around, "What are you doing?"

"Oh, sorry sir, Bill... Ben uh, Mr. Gruffly, but... there's somebody in that room."

Rubbing my arm, I continued stuttering while he inspected the conference room. "Sir, I realise I'm new at this, but I'm pretty sure he can't be in there while the office is closed. I was just trying to..."

"Dude! That's your boss!" said Ben — gruffly — and then called out, pointing: "Sorry, Ron... new-guy!"

"O...kay, this is mildly embarrassing." I said quietly as the gentleman stood up and walked over towards me — passing from the dark conference room into the brighter office space.

It was Ronald Addha, Chief Inspector in this division of Imperial Intelligence — and my new boss. He was not as tall as I expected. His face was tan. He had short black hair and a kind of beard, or maybe he just hadn't shaved. His suit was fine but visibly worn-out.

"And by whom, may I ask, do I have the pleasure of being kicked-out of *my own office*?" he said with a grin.

"Uh... Dude Salter, sir." I replied, as my head shrunk between my shoulders. "And... uh... I'm really sorry about that."

"Ah, you're our new science expert." he said, "Well... no harm done, Mr. Salter. I understand you worked on the Arctic Array — that's quite an innovative place. And I heard that you came up with many new methods and mechanisms down there — blending theory with practice.

"It is precisely that kind of talent that I want to put to work here in our office. In fact, if you don't mind, I'd like to pick your brain about something."

"Alright." I said.

"Now picture this: A ship load of newly discovered antiquities from far-away, arrives at an imperial research centre and warehouse to be cleaned, restored and studied. We're talking about thousands of historical items, including pottery, writings, engravings, and ancient devices. Some of these were very advanced — even for our time — and particularly important to the empire.

Then, in the space of just a few days, one item after another suffers some sort of accident, until they are all either shattered, crushed, burned or otherwise ruined. – What would you say about that?"

"Whoa!" I said, "Um, I'd say you've got a very clumsy staff!"

"Ha! I assure you, the staff is highly qualified. But it gets better." he continued, "When the staff members were questioned, they all began to forget everything about what they were working on before it was destroyed. And the more they were questioned, the more they forgot. It was almost as if the questions were erasing the answers! – Now, what would say about *that*?"

"Uh, wow! I'd say you've got some kind of conspiracy on your hands!"

"That was our impression as well." he said. "But our analysts found that none of the staff would benefit from lying. And after several medical examinations, it was confirmed that they all really did suffer from extensive memory loss.

"Mr. Salter, it is simply the most baffling case we've ever seen! What kind of mechanism could do such a thing? – This is something I'm hopeful you can help us with." he said.

But all I could do was shake my head slowly.

"Well," he continued, "needless to say I'm sure you'll be very much appreciated here."

"Oh, thank you, sir." I said breathing a sigh of relief. I was so worried about making a fool out of myself.

"Tell me something else," he continued "are you familiar with the type of *gravitron* described in *Echoes of the Aeonian Rift* or in *The Legend of the Sages*?"

"Um, uh... is that... like... a bar... or something?" I said sheepishly.

He didn't react. He and Ben just stared at me.

A few women – trying hard not to laugh – gathered their things from their desks and left the office, closing the door behind them.

"All right." he said, quietly chuckling and he pointed at something on a table, "Ben, give him some homework."

I then felt the blunt, deflating force of a heavy book shoved against my ribs.

"Oh." I said, as I recovered my breath, "...Thank you, sir."

"This research should hold you for tonight!" said Mr. Gruffly.

"Well, actually, tonight I'm dining out with my family and some relatives." I said, "You know, to celebrate this – my new job."

"Family?" asked Mr. Addha.

"Yes, I have a wife and a kid. It's really great. But don't worry, sir, it won't interfere with my work. – I promise! – I mean, at least not before... you know... closing time." I said with a chuckle.

They didn't laugh, though.

I probably should've just said goodnight at that point. But no. "Um...Do you have a family, Mr. Addha?"

Mr. Gruffly looked worriedly at Mr. Addha, as if I had just said something terrible.

There was a pause. "Um... no." he replied quietly, almost in a whisper, and folded his hands behind his back.

Mr. Gruffly was looking at me with the eyes of death, as if telling me to shut up, but at the moment I just didn't get it.

"Oh, well you should, sir." I continued, "There's nothing warmer or more happifying than having your own family to come home to. I mean, it really gives meaning to..."

"Enjoy your dinner, Mr. Salter." interrupted Mr. Gruffly.

"Oh, yes. Well, goodnight, then, sir... and sir." I said.

I grabbed my briefcase and ducked out of there as quickly as I could, and with what little dignity I had left.

And *that* was my first day at work...

— D. E. Salter

Two grey metal doors lit up cool-white, and silently slid open. A small group of people walked hurriedly out of the elevator and out of sight. A tall, young man in a brown suit stepped out as well, carrying a briefcase in one hand, and a large thick book, awkwardly in the other. The glowing white doors closed behind him with a soft click and grew dark.

There were several dozen elevators arranged in an inward-facing circle, with a few wide openings leading out to a much larger outer lobby. Mr. Salter stood at the centre of the circle for a moment, then remembered which way to go.

There was a crowd of people leaving on the far side of the lobby, but on his side it was quiet. The over-head lights dimmed, and an organic blue-green glow came up through the shiny floor. The sound of his footsteps echoed through the spacious lobby.

He stopped. Some movement behind some potted trees had caught his attention. But there was nothing. – Just a faint humming sound. Then a little bird suddenly flew out and over his head as he ducked down. "Gah! Whoa!" He watched it fly to another potted tree in a darker area of the lobby. "Oh! ...Darn nerves!" he said under his breath, "Relax, Dude!" he said to himself.

He was so tense coming in earlier that day that it hadn't occurred to him where he was standing. Then, a feeling of awe came over him as he looked up. He couldn't believe his eyes. Part of the ceiling above him was more than 50 stories high! There were actually thin clouds high up in the lobby!

That round bank of elevators he'd just left was only one of several elevator banks, clustered in groups. Each bank was housed in one of several great round ivory-coloured columns near the centre of the lobby. The columns all got wider as they rose higher, merging gracefully together as they reached up to the ceiling.

A ramp led up from the outer lobby floor to a mezzanine that spiralled up the round transparent outer wall, widening with each loop, right up to the ceiling.

The air smelled sweet. Trees and gardens filled every area. In the dim light he could see there were even hanging gardens on the glass walls, up the mezzanine and up its support columns.

He backed into a copper railing, almost dropping the heavy book he was carrying. He turned around, looked down, and saw even more gardens planted in shiny black circular pods of different sizes, arranged neatly on a glowing sub-floor, which spiralled downward, underground into the darkness.

This was no lobby – it was an arboretum! It was so open and spacious that it took a leap of the imagination just to understand he was still indoors.

Finally, Mr. Salter walked out through a thick, metal and glass door that opened with a startling whoosh of air. The rain outside had died down a bit, and the night air was full of mist.

He started walking along a partially glass-covered sidewalk next to a busy street, lit from bright bluish-purple lamps suspended above, and soft orange curb-lamps down at the sides. A silver street-tram came humming along on tracks beside him and stopped to pick up a crowd of passengers. He got on as well.

As the tram whisked him away, he looked back and up at that colossal building he had just come from, still unable to grasp the enormity of what he was seeing.

He had forgotten that this was not just some office building. The city had hundreds of thousands of buildings, but there were only a few dozen like this one. The top was blocked from view by rainclouds. In fact, on a night such as this one, the top would actually be far, far above the clouds, stretching from the ground up nearly three kilometres, like a giant needle, into the sky. This was no skyscraper – this was a *centroid*.

His eyes gazed upward, and his mouth hung open as the tram that carried him sped-up and disappeared down a fogy street, merging with the busy metropolis.

-PART 3-

The bustling streets resembled living veins and arteries woven together into an organic grid of movement, casting a glow of mixed orange and blue light up the sides of the buildings and onto the underside of the clouds.

Far above all the noise and movement there was only stillness and quietness. A slowly churning sea of clouds reflected the silver moonlight above, and those massive towers pierced through them, up into the starry night sky, like whales gasping for breath.

Mr. Gruffly sat down in his office, at his desk, with only a small silver lamp illuminating the surface. He held a slender telephone to his ear. "Hey, Peachy, what took you so long?" he said to the person on the line. "Well sure, I understand. I'm in the business of being careful. So, what did you find out? ...Hold on."

He took a stylus from his inner jacket pocket and started writing on a light leaf. The translucent pages glowed with a yellowish hue as they captured and organized his notes.

"Wait. That's it? ...But we knew that already. What about its exact location at the moment they lost contact? – Its speed? – Its trajectory? ...Where would it have ended up? ...What about its transponder?

"What? ...I *know* it's classified! Why do you think I asked *you*? ...No, not because I was your *boss* years ago – it's because I know you're good. L... Listen. Listen..." he sighed, "This is *Ron* we're talking about."

Mr. Addha stood by a window in his darkened office, looking down, his eyes fixed on a small aircraft flying below as it descended into the clouds.

Light from the common area of the office was coming through his open door. A shadow appeared in the doorway.

"How did everything go in Flagstone today, sir?"

"Hmm... As well as you'd expect, I guess, knowing me." chuckled Mr. Addha, with a touch of self-pity, and still facing the window.

"I know we've been on the fence about this, Ben... but I think we should stick to our defensive stance at the hearing tomorrow. Things just don't add up. Why would Lord Sage throw away everything? What would he have to gain?"

"Alright," said Mr. Gruffly, "we'll do our best. Lord sage will need someone on his side anyway. Especially with Mr. Zoddoz leading the other team!"

"Oh, don't remind me!" he said shaking his head. "So, I heard you talking to Peachy just now. – Any news?"

"No." replied Mr. Gruffly, in almost a whisper, as if with a lump in his throat.

Mr. Addha closed his eyes and rubbed his forehead. "Well, you should get home, Ben. I don't want to keep Margie up, waiting for you. And I definitely don't want her blaming *me* for it!"

Ben half smiled. "You'll be alright, then, sir?"

"Yeah."

"Okay...well, Goodnight then, sir." he said, as he started turning away.

Then he stopped. "Oh... you know... Margie and I were thinking about your father in his new home. He must be feeling terrible about all this as well. I just want to say, if you speak to him, tell him we said hello and we wish him all the best."

Mr. Addha nodded. "Thank you, Ben. It's been a while. But... I will."

~ ~ ~

Outside, above the clouds, the towering centroid stood like a guardian in the night. Its dark green skin contrasted against the silvery cloud tops. And, in the background, dozens more stood like solders keeping watch. Its round spiral shape gracefully tapered as it rose to dizzying heights. There was this glowing, bluish-purple haze near its top-spires, which were arranged in a ring, like a crown on the head of a king.

At the top, just below the base of its spires, there was an outward structure like a short tree-branch or a small fin, with several others like it below and around the sides. Each one actually housed a spacious, multi-level observation deck, enclosed with glass. Inside, a man got off a small elevator and was climbing some stairs.

Above the fin, a small service hatch opened onto the top. A man in a suit came out into the cool crisp night air. The spires above him hummed and crackled, as they pulled the electricity right out of the air.

His tie flapped wildly in the wind as he climbed down some steep metal steps, onto a metal grating above the observation deck. The whole structure seemed to shake and sway in the wind.

He grasped the railing firmly as he looked down at the moon-lit clouds more than a kilometre below.

With his face pale, eyes watery, and feeling sick to his stomach, Mr. Addha began wondering exactly how high up he was. He could feel a cold teardrop from his eye roll down his cheek. He felt it just hang there for a second. Then he felt it drop away and watched with horror as it vanished into the abyss below, imagining, as he watched, that it was actually *he* who was falling.

He let out a small gasp and backed away from the railing, clinching his teeth out of regret. A strong gust of wind blew him back and he stumbled backwards against the stair-rail and clutched his chest as if his heart were giving out. He sat down on the stairs, weeping from the pain. He closed his eyes and took deep breaths to calm himself. He knew what was happening – it was a panic attack.

Suddenly there was a loud, startling sound of jet engines over his head. A large silver coloured regional star liner passed over him and ascended higher and higher into the sky, with its blinking lights, sharp nose, broad and gracefully swept-back wings, and a sort of disk at the centre. At the back, a faint blue flame could be seen through a wide engine-vent below its tail. Then its engines fell completely silent as it sped away, effortlessly, into the sky.

Trying to breathe calmly, he kept watching its blinking red lights until it had just about faded into the blackness of night. He watched it as it joined hundreds of other ships high above the atmosphere with their strobing lights. And he saw the brief, random white flashes of new ships arriving from faraway worlds, like shooting stars.

Seen through the clear night air at the top of that tower, thousands of stars came into focus for him, spread out across the sky like a tent, and from one horizon to the other, the great Milky Way.

He sat there on those cold metal steps, breathing deeply, pondering, with his eyes fixed on the stars – not even feeling the cold wind up there, high above the sea of moon-lit clouds.

Elsewhere, down below, off a busy little brick-paved street, at a corner dining spot with candles and string-lights, a young man in a brown suit, carrying a briefcase and a thick book, was warmly welcomed inside with kisses and pats on the back. He sat down to a table surrounded by family and friends, as wine was poured in a glass for him.

A child seated next to him pointed at the huge book he was carrying around. He put it on the table in front of the child and told him it was his homework. The child's mouth dropped open, and everybody laughed. And he began telling them all about his first day at work.

And elsewhere, and a little later, in a brownstone house on a quiet city street, an older man in a raincoat came home to his wife of many years. He gave her a kiss on the forehead while she sat on a couch, reading a book and listening to the calm music of classical composers.

As he put his coat away and poured himself a drink, she asked him about a dear friend of theirs. He sat down on his recliner and shook his head. – The news wasn't good.

And yet elsewhere, and later still, in a dark apartment, a young worn-out gentleman with an old worn-out suit, sat in his armchair, hunched over with his head cradled in his hands. Raindrops on the balcony window glistened with the city lights behind them. Shadows dripped down his face as he looked up at a timepiece on the wall. It was half-past-midnight. He seemed bothered by all the lights outside, as if they were brighter than usual for this hour.

He got up and walked over to the balcony window. The cold glass fogged over from his breath as he closed the yellow drapes. He stopped and opened them again and turned around to look again at the wall behind him.

Dozens of faces smiled at him from inside their picture frames: a couple just married, a baby, a toddler, another baby, two toddlers, the parents with the children, the grandparents and, oh, so many friends. And hanging among all these was the timepiece he had just consulted. And inscribed over the silver dial were the words: "*To Ronald and Deborah Addha, the happiest couple of the Aeon.*" His wireless gave three low beeps. And again, three low beeps, and again ...and again. But he didn't move. He just stood there grief-stricken and full of sorrow – staring at his wall of memories – reliving a past that was dripping with shadows of the rain.

3

THE HAZY
LIGHT OF DAWN

*I*n the small hours of the morning, on a darkened road, by the light of the full moon, a cloaked horseman came along riding. He stopped near the top of a hill to visit a once-familiar place. Off to the right, up a twisted and long-abandoned road, the great house sat in ruins – a burned and charred hulk of stone, brick and mortar. Old broken walls and towering crooked chimneys stood blackened against the starry night-sky. The horseman removed his brown hood from over his head. His aged yet vibrant face looked around with astonishment at the moon-lit ruins.

What happened to the proud stately home that had once stood in this place? He seemed as though he knew but was amazed just the same. He took one last look 'round, then continued on his way, directing his black horse forward – forward up the darkened road.

Its hoofs rose high with each step, stomping the ground. Its wild black eyes reflected the dim starry light, and its nostrils gave off breath of curling white steam in the cool crisp air of night.

Once over a hill, the gleaming night-sea came into view sparkling under the blue moonlight. Scattered white rocks punctuated the rolling black landscape and the sandy strand beneath the foaming waves.

The windswept hills were both peaceful and haunting, as cold howling gusts blew from every direction across the slopes and fields of tall wild grass. The grey and black stalks swayed in unison, like waves in the wind.

And on the slope of another hill, off in the distance, the silhouette of a small black stone house perched like an owl, overlooking the sea.

— J. B. Kendal

～～～

YEARS POST RIFT: 4143+001/516: RYATTII DIFFERENTIAL
THE LANDINGS, NEW RYATTII

He didn't think it was a nightmare at the time. The sound of quick-paced footsteps overhead roused him from his sleep. It was still dark outside, and way too early in the morning for so much noise. It sounded like someone was looking for something urgently. Back and forth, this way and that way, 'round and 'round — the heavy-footed character upstairs simply would not quit. So much noise! Mr. Addha grabbed a second pillow and put it over his face. He needed to sleep. He was too tired for this.

Then, suddenly, he sat up with a ghostly feeling. He realized that the rooms overhead were actually the upper floor of *his own apartment*! Who-in-the-world was in his apartment? He sat up slowly – his muscles tensed, ears tuned, eyes open wide and fixed on the ceiling – following the sound of the footsteps on the hardwood floor upstairs. He tried to figure out if he was still asleep, dreaming, or might the sound actually be coming from somewhere else.

He needed a weapon. He went to the dresser, grabbed his holster, pulled out his silver charge-pistol with one hand, and with the other hand, pulled a small lever on the top to switch it on. Narrow vents on its sides glowed blue and let out a brief hissing sound as the air around it became electrified.

He held his pistol tightly at his side as he left the bedroom and quietly made his way into the living room, towards the staircase. The noise upstairs stopped, and so did he. And he wondered if he really had been dreaming but couldn't be sure.

Slowly, silently, toes first, step by step, he climbed up the stairs. One of the wooden steps creaked loudly. He ducked down, expecting a reaction. But nothing happed. In the upstairs hallway, dim blue light from outside entered through a small window at the end of it.

He approached the first doorway to the side, pushing open the door with his foot as he stood behind the doorframe. He clinched his teeth trying not to let the door creak. But there was only the undisturbed, rose-coloured serenity of a little girl's empty bedroom and some of her toys. And across the hallway there was only the empty, pale-blue bedroom of a playful little boy. Even the closets were empty.

The third room was a half-finished nursery – undisturbed for some time. The forth was an office in the midst of being transformed into a master bedroom, though it was far from finished. Dusty boxes were neatly stacked against one wall. The upstairs bathroom was also empty.

At that point, he realized it must've been a nightmare, and shook his head. He was relieved but needed air. He went downstairs through the living room, still feeling on edge and looking around him, nervously.

A shiny black piano sat lonely in one corner, and a violin leaned against the wall behind some armchairs in another. And dim, hazy blue light came in through the glass sliding-doors that lead outside onto the terrace.

The cool air outside smelled fresh and damp with mist. The plants around the terrace-railing were all covered with dewdrops. He breathed in deeply as he took in the sweeping view. It was the thing he liked most about that apartment.

The great city out there in the distance sat sleeping, wrapped in a vast blanket of fog, lit-up icy blue with the early-morning light. The very tops of the kilometres-high centroids began gleaming brightly with golden-yellow light as they caught the first rays of sun from far over the horizon to the left. And to the right, two bright stars were setting, like small flickers of candlelight – the *Aerii Sisters*, distant suns, one yellow and the other blue.

But then, it occurred to him: if there ever had been an intruder, he or she could have escaped onto another terrace. His building was slanted back, so that up every two stories there was an outdoor terrace, set back about ten meters from the one below it. He looked over the railing at the neighbouring terraces a short distance away, then down, and then up and behind.

As he turned to look up he jumped back and let out a small noise as his eyes met those of an older woman and her husband, standing on their own terrace, two stories above him.

"Are you alright down there, Mr. Addha?" she asked. They looked disturbed at the sight of him. They had been sipping their coffee, apparently waiting to watch the sunrise in a few minutes.

"Of course!" he replied. And then he realized how ridiculous he must have looked — standing out there bare-foot, in his night-clothes, with his sweaty hand clutching a shiny charge-pistol.

There was nothing to be said. He just smiled.

As he walked back inside, he heard the man's voice saying with a chuckle: "It must be the equinox!"

He closed the sliding doors behind him with a click and rubbed his forehead. "What's wrong with me?" he thought, as he went back to his bedroom. He switched off the charge-pistol and threw it down.

It was still early, but he couldn't go back to sleep. He looked at his mobile. A small, orange light was blinking slowly. The slim, round device fit neatly in his hand, and the shiny round screen came to life. He had missed a com last night at $00^h 31^m$. It was Ben Gruffly.

A blue button appeared on the screen. It turned white, sensing that he wanted to hear it...

Ron, it's Ben.

Admin just told me there's a problem with the hand-off tonight. None of the far-side cities confirmed any data transfer. And it's not just us, it's all of the Centroid offices. It looks like the place is going to be up and running all night. The good news is nothing's lost, just a lot of clerical catching-up to do. It's weird, I don't remember this ever happening before. Anyway, I'll see you tomorrow; I'll be there early.

-Bye.

Oh, yeah... and... Margie says thanks!

The screen went dark as he put it down and rubbed his eyes, remembering how he was feeling the night before. Then he touched-on the lamp. Something was missing from his nightstand.

He looked down at the floor, around and under his bed. And there it was – a small brown book – a journal written by some unknown person from an unknown place. He must have dropped it when he fell asleep. It was old – leather bound, with no writing on the cover. And inside, on the first page, there was only written the word: *Reminiscences.*

He held it quietly in his hands, staring at it, wondering if this was the source of his nightmare.

RECORDING OF RONALD ADDHA

Well, that was a strange day from the very beginning. That morning as usual, I took the tram to a favourite corner of mine. There was this place called Agatha's. It was just this little open-air café, you know, with small round tables and chairs on the sidewalk. The outer wall folded away and there was a bar inside with a large round screen behind it, with a woman announcing the news, and I could hear it from outside.

I liked the fact that I could enjoy a meal, be informed, and get my mind working – taking in the vibrant energy of the busy streets, the motorcars and trams, and people walking by, and the shop owners opening up their trades and crafts to the world.

That day, my mind was off to a slow start. I checked through my briefcase and took out this old journal and put it on the table, shaking my head at myself as I remembered how I got it.

It was about a week earlier. During one of my visits to Lord Sage, while I was waiting to see him, I had ventured into his personal work area – his private study – full of writing projects, complex drawings and models he had been working on, and I began to photograph everything in that place.

Well, it was only a brief episode of boldness however, and my nerves soon took over. I saw this little book sitting on his desk, grabbed it, stuffed it in my jacket pocket, and got out of there before he noticed where I'd gone.

And so, here it was, in my hand. I wasn't sure what I could learn from it. So far, all there was of any relevance was just the name: *Sage*.

I looked up as I heard the news announcer, on that large round screen inside, mentioning the data-outage of the night before.

And then the sharp professional looking woman, with long straight black hair and a red suit introduced another story...

ARCHIVED NEWS RECORDING

<< ...It has now been more than a month since the mysterious disappearance of the *Dawn* – a regional star liner that vanished during a routine flight to Aerii.

Officials of the Aerii Port Authority said that the Dawn never made contact, and that she stopped transmitting her location around the same time that she would've begun reversing engines – the riskiest part of any gravity-driven voyage.

They added that, since then, no signals have been received from any personal wireless devices that would've been on board.

The Dawn was one of the few Seneca-class star liners still in service, built and flown by the Vern Rymann Aerospace Company to several destinations throughout the Tri-Systems.

The Seneca-class design – known for its distinctive gracefully swept-back wings – was actually the first passenger spacecraft to use a fluid-state gravity-engine. It is now the oldest design still in use by that company since their discontinuation of the heavier and enormous rotor-type engines of long ago.

A spokesman for the company said they are certain that age was not a factor, and that no other crafts have had any major problems.

In the meantime, the two Imperial Jammers that sped out to the area where the Dawn is believed to have disappeared, still have found no debris or evidence of any kind.

There were 287 people on board, including 18 crew members... >>

To my ears, everything else she said just seemed to fade away into a garbled noise, and I felt numb. I had been trying so hard to forget. My mobile rang-out with several low beeps. – Someone was trying to call me. But I ignored it. – I just looked down, staring at the ring on my finger.

Through the muffled sounds and blurry surroundings, I had noticed a figure standing off to the side. I wiped my eyes. – They were a bit watery. Then someone walked up to me from behind. A beige raincoat brushed my arm. And an older man's voice calmly asked: "May I join you, Mr. Addha?"

-PART 2-

The old pale gentleman stood there quietly, gazing down at me with his grey eyes from beneath a white brimmed hat.

"Of course... Lord Sage!" I said with astonishment.

He seated himself and put his hat down on another chair while I moved my plate and my books and papers to make room for him. The silly fork slid off my plate and clanged against the stone patio floor. Lord Sage patiently folded his hands on the table, as I bent over to pick up the fork.

Before I could return it to my plate, a tall thin man – the owner of the café – was standing at the table, having already brought me a clean one.

"Oh... thank you!"

"Not at all, sir." he said, handing it to me with a curt smile from beneath a strangely trimmed moustache. He turned to Lord Sage. "And would you care for anything, sir?"

"Oh, yes, green tea, if you please." he replied, nodding graciously, as the man turned and left.

I sat pensively for just a moment with my fist to my nose, wondering what Lord Sage was doing here. But I quickly changed my posture as I realized how I looked.

"I believe you have something of mine." he said with a smirk.

"Um..., yes." I stuttered. I had forgotten that that old journal was still sitting on the table in plain sight.

I put it in my jacket pocket and tried to play it off as officially-sounding as I could, "I *do* intend to return it to you as soon as I've finished examining it. I'm sorry for not asking first, but, *if* there's information I need, then I cannot risk being *denied* it. – I'm sure you understand."

"It's no trouble, young man. Besides, there's nothing in that book that you can use, at least not at this time."

I glanced down at the papers I had assembled, and then up at him again. "My lord, I'm curious. I told you yesterday that we're scheduled to meet later this morning. So... why are you here at this table with me now... and how did you even know I would be here?"

He looked down. His lips tightened, as if he knew the effect his words would have on me. Then he looked up. "When information is not available by normal means, I will still learn just what I need to know for the task at hand – nothing more, nothing less. – I am not at liberty to discuss my source."

His cryptic words stunned me, like an electric eel that stuns its prey. And all I could do was blink my eyes.

Lord Sage paused as the owner returned with a cup of hot water, a little ball of green tealeaves floating in it, and a little open jar of honey. He leaned forward slightly over the cup and breathed-in the scent of the tea, then picked it up delicately, sipped it carefully, and put it down gently. "And as for my *reasons* for being here now," he continued, "I believe it would be less dangerous for you to ask your questions in a ... *neutral* setting, like this."

"Less *dangerous*?" I said, leaning forward and looking in his eyes: "– For who? – For you? But, you know I wouldn't let them use that machine on you. That thing is only used on hardened low-life criminals to catch them in their lies."

He raised his eyebrows dismissively as he warmed his bony hands around the little teacup. I sat back and sighed to myself. I wanted to defend him, but he was irritating me.

Here sat a man who was used to making the rules – in fact, a whole system of rules. But he had actually created a monster – a huge clockwork of heavy wheels that even he couldn't stop.

"Well," I said, "you know you still have to appear in court today. With such an accusation of destroying information and government-owned artefacts, interfering with imperial business – in fact, undermining the empire – I'm afraid there's no choice."

He looked off to the side. His eyes seemed to wander down the streets of another city, in another time. "No, Mr. Addha... there are many ways to find the truth about the past. But this great imperial machine is too big and clumsy to find it. Like an elephant in a flower garden, with every step it takes, it demolishes yet another useful clue."

I leaned forward. "Excuse me, sir, but isn't it *you* who has demolished these 'useful clues'? All these years you've carefully collected and catalogued every trace from the old colonies of Ryattii. But now, when others try to use this information, it suddenly and inexplicably disappears or is ruined beyond any usefulness! – We even had to bring in a science expert to work with our team of analysts, just to figure out how you did it and how extensive the damage is!"

But he shook his head. "Mr. Addha, you are treading in areas beyond your understanding. There are laws of physics at play here that escape even the most advanced scientists."

"What do you mean? And how could that possibly have anything to do with this?"

He leaned back, he was extremely uncomfortable. "Let me try a different approach. What do you know about physical laws that come into play when someone has a message to send?"

I was annoyed. But reluctantly I answered: "Alright. Well, I know that a message cannot be moved any faster than the speed of light."

"Indeed. But we've side-stepped that problem these days with our twin-lattice technology. Your mobile uses this technology." He said, pointing at my mobile on the table, "Instead of *moving* information, it is simply *duplicated* instantaneously, regardless of location. – The little atoms inside of two mobiles will behave as if they're right next to each other, even though they could actually be *worlds apart*.

"Now," he continued, "what I am talking about, Mr. Addha, is an obscure set of physical laws that actually control *who* may know exactly *what*, and be able to *act* on that information, and at what *time*.

"And here is where it gets interesting. When one of these laws is violated, nature will try to correct that violation – sometimes with inexplicable phenomenon. And the more severely these laws are violated, the more drastic the correcting effect will be."

Honestly, at this point my eyes were glazing over a bit, but I could understand where he was going. "Lord Sage, that is ridiculous! Do you honestly expect me to believe that all of this destruction and lost information is to be blamed on some obscure science?"

I was getting loud. I stopped for a moment to lower my voice, as other people around us were getting uncomfortable. "You should hear what other people say about you, sir. – It's embarrassing. All of my peers think that you're either a criminal, or a..."

He held the warm teacup to his face, about to take another sip. "...Or a what?" he asked.

"...Or a fake." I said, ashamed of my words as they came out of my mouth. "And some have even said that you're *both*. But I've always defended you. And I've paid dearly for it... and I continue to pay. And quite frankly ... I'm tired of it."

-PART 3-

Lord Sage put down his teacup. He glanced down at all the documents that I had put together – the charts and maps, the photographs, and the testimonials. Then he looked at my jacket, into which I had put that old journal. "Was there anything else that you took from my study, Mr. Addha?"

"I don't know what you mean, my lord." I said, shaking my head.

"I *mean* ... was there an artefact or a device that you may have touched, perhaps, out of curiosity? – Even for a moment?"

"No. Why? Is something missing?"

Lord Sage looked at me with tired but intense eyes. He seemed to analyse me for any signs of dishonesty. I'm not sure what he was seeing, but I didn't flinch. I stared right back at him with the same intensity. I think, at that time, he must have felt like someone who was losing control of his life.

"Do you think I don't know what you're after, Mr. Addha?" continued Lord Sage, "Or, did you forget the quest of your childhood? ...You asked me a question, the first time you met me. Do you remember?"

"My lord, please, I don't understand. What are you talking about, sir?"

"You were only a child, on a class outing, visiting my house as you would some museum. Your teacher gathered you and your classmates around my chair in the same room that you sat in yesterday. She told you I had written many of your schoolbooks. Then she explained the role I played in historical preservation and invited you all to ask me your questions.

"One by one, the little children asked me about this thing and that, about why that is like this, and whether I knew any of their relatives.

"And then it was *your* turn. And do you know what you said? You stood up, looked me in the eyes and said: 'What happened to the world that came before our world? Why did that world end? Will the same thing happen to our world?'

"Well, everyone in your class was silent. Your poor teacher didn't know what to do. And I sat back in my chair, dumbfounded. No one had ever asked me such a thing. And I wondered to myself: 'What kind of a man... is inside that little child?'"

Lord Sage leaned forward and looked me in my eyes. "Well, have you found your answers yet, Mr. Addha?

"You *do* remember that day, don't you?" he continued, "What happened? Other people didn't feel comfortable around you, *did* they?

"It's not really as though no one else had ever asked such things. They just went about it *differently*. They were *careful*. They used the right *words*. They spoke to the right *people*. They dug around all the right *places*.

"But what about *you*? What scared you off? Perhaps you've noticed the pattern of fear around you. The higher up you go, the scarier it gets, doesn't it? People start to realize they've got much more to lose, don't they?"

As he was speaking, I noticed he was sweating, and he patted down his face with a cloth. "My Lord," I said quietly, "do you have something to lose?"

He didn't answer. Instead, he put down the cloth and picked up his hat, breathing heavily. "Excuse me for my delirium, Mr. Addha, but I'm feeling a bit *ill* at the moment. Would you mind if we moved our conversation to my motorcar? My driver is standing-by at the corner, just up there."

"Yes, of course, my Lord!" I said as I helped him up from his seat. He took a short black cylinder from his coat pocket and unfolded it into a cane. His driver seemed to understand the sign and ran over to walk him back to the cream-coloured motorcar.

While I gathered my things I waved-over an attendant in the café, who came running, bringing a copper-coloured light-board, which I signed with my finger to pay favour.

After he left, my eyes stopped on something on the table – that cup of tea Lord Sage had been drinking, with that little ball of green tea leaves still in it. 'Might that've been poisoned?' I wondered.

I looked around. I didn't want to linger and draw attention. So, I threw a napkin over the cup and tucked it in the crook of my arm as I picked up my brief case and left.

As I carried my things to the motorcar, I had failed to notice that, among all the noise and movement on the street, a black motorcar had stopped back a little further up the street.

With the window lowered, the driver, thin faced with slick hair and wearing sunglasses, had all the while been taking photographs of me with Lord Sage – talking, eating and leaving. Then the window went up as the driver prepared to follow us.

Inside the café, the owner took the light-board from his attendant, walked over to the doorway and stood there, watching indifferently as we drove off.

The motorcar's interior was very fine – black leather with chrome trim. The ride was smooth and quiet; I hardly felt it moving as it rolled along on its well-tuned roller-belt.

I placed the teacup with the napkin over it on the seat next to me. Then I took a small metal case out from my jacket pocket and opened it. A tiny glass tube slipped out into my other hand. I removed the napkin, opened the tube, and started carefully pouring a trickle of tee into the tube.

Lord Sage shook his head as he watched me. "Mr. Addha, you seem to have a knack for carrying *out* more than you carry *in*!"

"I couldn't risk losing this evidence, my Lord. I have every intention of returning the cup when I'm finished." I explained. "Don't you realize that you might've been poisoned?"

"I seriously doubt that. – At such a random time and place? Meeting you there was a last-minute decision. How could anyone have known that I would...?" Then he paused. His face had become pale. And he just stared up at the buildings as we drove along.

Really, I was annoyed but tried not to show it. I sealed the tube. Then I put the cup with the tea leaves and the rest of the liquid in a small re-sealable plastic bag.

"Time is precious." I continued, as I put everything into my briefcase, "In just one second, a whole world of evidence can be gained or lost."

"...Yes." said Lord Sage, as he looked out his window and up at the glassy towers. "Believe me, Mr. Addha... I know."

— The Inevitable Quest
Interviews by Danae Southendorn

~~~

Gwithian, England
Saturday, April 26th, 1823

The sound of quick-paced footsteps, just outside their bedroom door, roused John from his sleep. It was still dark outside, too early in the morning for so much noise. It sounded like someone was searching for something urgently. Back and forth, this way and that way, 'round and 'round – the leather-booted character out in the hallway simply would not quit. And outside in the shed by the house, the dogs kept on barking. So much noise! John grabbed a second pillow and put it over his face. He needed to sleep. He was too tired for this.

Then, suddenly, he sat up with a ghostly feeling; 'It must be an intruder!' he thought. He got up slowly in the bed, his muscles tensed, his eyes opened wide, fixed on the door, and his ears tuned, following the sound of the footsteps on the hardwood floors. He tried to figure out if he was still asleep, dreaming, or if the sound might instead be something else. Then it stopped.

"What's wrong?" asked Mary, as she rolled over in the bed.

"Didn't you hear that?" whispered John.

"Hear what?"

"All that noise, didn't you *hear* it?"

Mary rubbed her eyes, yawned, and smiled: "John, my dear…, the last noise I remember hearing was the sound of someone downstairs late last night, shouting at the window like a crazed lunatic!"

John understood she was joking about him – but he was not amused. Now Mary looked at him and saw that he was genuinely afraid. The sound came back, and they both heard it. Someone was running out of the bedroom across the hall, down the stairs, and out the front door.

John jumped out of bed and in a blur grabbed his glasses and housecoat, and his musket off the wall. As he opened their bedroom door he turned and shouted in a whisper to Mary: "Find Emily! Hide with her under her bed!"

The room across the hall was the boy's room. He burst in to check on them. The two younger boys were startled and just waking up. But David's bed was empty.

"Where's David?" he screamed, "Who was in here?"

But he didn't wait for an answer. He ran down the hall and down the stairs. The front door hung wide open. Then, wielding his musket, he ran out, bare foot, into the cold dark misty air of the early morning.

He looked around. There was someone running away, down the strand, along the sea. John ran out onto a sandy ridge overlooking the seashore and shouted at the top of his voice: "David! David!"

John kept running along the ridge, shouting: "Stop! Come back! Please!"

But whoever it was, they were already too far off, and he lost sight of them.

Finally, after running-on for a quarter mile, out of breath, he threw down his musket in frustration. He clutched his forehead with his sweaty hands, and fell to his knees, gasping for breath, and saying: "Oh! ...Oh, God! ...I've lost him!"

Suddenly as he looked up, his eyes became fixed on something out at sea. And his face became white. Out there, anchored under a full moon, with her sails neatly folded and tied-up, shrouded in the dark blue morning mist, on the calm glassy waters of Carbis Bay, sat there quietly a great wooden tall ship of war.

Through the haze, it was too far to make-out any identifying features. Yet, in his heart, John seemed to recognize it. But he shook his head in disbelief. It was as if an old relic from his past had just been resurrected, and was standing before him now, to claim his share. And he trembled. Impossible! He thought. – The Phantom! – The very ship that had eluded him in his dreams, now sat there, motionless, as if immune to the passing of time. And it seemed to be daring him, taunting him, to chase after it once more, out there into the hazy light of dawn.

4

GRUMMAN

The dogs outside, tied up in the shed, barked and howled as if to voice the family's disgust over what had happened. Inside, however, not a word was spoken. The morning sun was now peaking in through the windows. His wife gathered some foodstuffs and put them in a sack. The children huddled on the stairs, watching their father as he marched back and forth through the house collecting his things. – As he put on his leather boots, his gloves, his coat and brimmed hat. – As he gathered his musket with his shot and gunpowder.

John looked and sounded like a soldier – his boots clamouring against the wooden floor. He marched hurriedly to the front door, stopped and looked back at Mary and the children. They nodded in unison, as if to say 'March-on, bring our David home!' He turned around, pulled the latch forcefully and swung open the creaky front door.

He had not so much as taken one step outside, when suddenly, he came face to face with a big black horse's mouth. The beast grunted and chuckled at him, sniffed and snorted at him, and stomped the wet grass with its heavy hoof, staring him down with its big black eyes.

Its rider, wearing a reddish-brown cloak, removed his hood. And with a serious but pleasant expression on his aged yet vibrant face, he leaned forward, bowed his head slightly, and said with an educated yet tactful accent: "Good morning, Mr. Kendal."

John jumped back as he shouted in surprise: "Grumman!" And in a snap he pointed his musket up at the man. The family inside gasped, and the three dogs outside barked ever more, pulling at their cords. Little Caleb screamed-out: "It's that bad man!" But his mother restrained him.

The great black stallion, feeling uncomfortable, whined and shuffled nervously side to side. "It's alright. It's alright." the horseman whispered in its ear as he calmed and quieted the animal, patting it on its neck.

Still pointing his musket, ever protective, John said with a commanding voice: "Get down off that thing!" The cloaked horseman, although annoyed, accepted his authority for the moment and dismounted.

Just then little Caleb slipped free of his mother's grip, though she tried to stop him, and he burst out the door. "I'll save you, papa!" he screamed as he ran out on his little feet to the shed by the side of the house and loosened one of the dogs.

"No, Caleb!" screamed his father. But it was too late. The snarling hound wriggled loose from his cord and took-off running towards the intruder.

"Get him! Get him!" cheered Caleb, jumping and clapping his hands. But, perceiving the black stallion as a bigger threat, the hound ran towards it instead and bit down hard on its front leg. The horse reared-up on its hind legs, neighing furiously, and took-off galloping towards the sea with the hound chasing after it.

John whistled loudly, "Stop it! Get back here!" he ordered, with his voice echoing across the strand. The dog obeyed finally and returned with its head low to the ground and ears towards its master.

Caleb sat quietly with the dog, wondering which of the two was in bigger trouble.

But the black horse just kept galloping away wildly, veering left down the strand, beyond the dunes towards Carbis Bay, and out of sight. "Ah..." said Grumman, under his breath, "...charming."

〜〜〜

John returned his attention to the now horseless Mr. Grumman: "Do you dare return here to bid me 'good morning' after kidnapping our David?"

Grumman looked stunned for a moment. "I beg your pardon?"

"Oh, drop your polite hypocrisy, Grumman! Did you really think we wouldn't hear you barging all through the house?"

"Forgive me, but I really have no idea what you're talking about."

John's face turned red. "David told us that you were looking for him yesterday! What have you to say about *that*?"

"What?" said Grumman imploringly, "I... I'm sorry, but... that's simply not... at all true."

"Well then, how is it that he described you to us, exactly?"

"It's... not possible."

"Yes, it *is* possible because you were sneaking around Hayle yesterday looking for him, and he *saw* you!"

"No... I'm telling you, I've only just arrived!"

"Oh, really then! Well, let's try a different approach. Tell me, did you not arrive here on His Majesty's Ship, anchored out there?" John shouted, pointing out at the bay.

"Yes." Grumman replied cautiously.

"And are there not, at this very moment, some two hundred service men out there, waiting on you to carry out your orders?"

"Well... yes."

"And with such a show of force, are you not here looking for David right now?"

"Yes, but..."

"Then tell me, man, why should I trust you, and why should I spare your life now that you've invaded our house and kidnapped our child!"

But he held out his hand and said firmly: "Now, hold-on! Just cool your head off, Mr. Kendal... Now, as a general rule, there are two things I don't do: I don't go barging through private homes, and I most certainly don't go around kidnapping people...

"Now... His Majesty has been most gracious in granting me the use of one of his vessels. But it is only because he believes me so trustworthy, and my purpose so noble."

John slowly lowered the musket and rubbed the back of his neck. He turned his head and looked at his family just inside the open door. Caleb had snuck back inside as well.

"Philip," he said to the other older boy, "did you see this man in the house this morning?"

"No, Papa." he said quietly, "Actually, I didn't see anybody."

John, feeling both relief and a renewed feeling of despair, looked down. And his eyes fell upon his faithful dog, sitting by his feet, panting with watchful eyes, ever ready to protect and obey. He shook his head and said in a low voice: "...Forgive me."

He meant it, of course, for Mr. Grumman, but in his heart it was for David and his long-lost father, to whom he had made a solemn promise which, it seemed, he had now failed to keep.

"I don't believe you would be so foolish to return here after doing such a malicious thing. But…" John paused, adjusting his glasses and looking at Grumman's face in the morning sunlight to see his reaction; his look was concerned yet calm; his intense silvery eyes didn't flinch as he waited for John to finish.

"But… somehow, I just know you must've had something to do with it."

"Mr. Kendal, I assure you, I have only the most respectable intentions…"

But John had had enough. He was wasting time. "Enough." he said: "Please leave us. As you can see, we have a crisis in our family, and I have the most urgent business to attend to."

John bent down to pick up his things. "And I believe that you, sir, have a runaway-horse to recover." he said as he walked past him, taking up the road west to Hayle.

He whistled to his dog, and the hound immediately jumped up and followed him.

"You're right, Mr. Kendal…" said Grumman.

John stopped and turned around, listening.

"I'm afraid that… I *do* have some… responsibility… in this."

John stood motionless, waiting. Grumman took a step toward him, "But I assure you, my responsibility is not because of any malice or any bad thing that I have done, but because of something I have *failed* to do… And I feel compelled to help you find him."

John looked at him with narrow eyes. He didn't trust anything Grumman said and felt very uncomfortable at the thought of travelling with him. But, at least, he thought, he could keep an eye on him; and it seemed better than leaving the stranger anywhere near his house or his family. "Alright." he said, raising his hand in the direction of the road.

Grumman stepped forward to follow him. John looked at his wife, Mary, standing in the front doorway with their children behind her. Their eyes locked. He gave her a little nod of his head. She understood.

Grumman also turned for a moment, looking back at the house – back at Mary as she closed the creaky wooden door with a slam and bolted it shut.

-PART 2-

Viewed from high above, the great city of New Ryattii wrapped around the busy harbour and spread out from one horizon to the other. The mass of thousands of glassy towers sparkling with beams of golden sun looked like a radiant field of wild grass, coated with morning dew.

Off in the distance, the Upper and Lower Centroid Districts were unmistakable. Jutting up some two or three kilometres above the city, the massive centroids completely dominated the skyline as super-skyscrapers, reaching up like giant glassy splinters of greenish-yellow light.

An organic green colour graced the tops of most of the other buildings throughout the city, as well as their many terraces and balconies. It was a hanging forest of trees, planted a hundred meters above the ground, interconnected and patched together with sky-bridges and walk-ways, forming a sort of open lattice. It was like a huge park suspended far above the city streets.

Down below, the morning sun glistened between the glass buildings, illuminating the busy streets and tramways of smooth, unending movement. And among all the motion and variety of vehicles, a cream-coloured motorcar, elegant yet sleek, confidently navigated the vast grid-work of streets.

Running silently on its roller-belt of rubber and steel, it came to a gentle stop near the centre of the Old Founders District, in front of an ancient looking building made of white polished granite, with grand columns and soaring arches which were rebuilt to support a great dome of glass and iron.

The driver got out to open the rear door by the sidewalk. Mr. Addha hesitated for a moment and turned to Lord Sage. "It's still a bit early. Are you coming, my Lord? Or will you wait?" But the old man just sat there in his beige raincoat and white brimmed hat, staring up at the buildings. Mr. Addha said nothing more and started to get out of the motorcar.

"How much longer will you pretend?" said Lord Sage.

Mr. Addha stopped and turned around. "I beg your pardon?"

"...How much longer will you pretend that nothing's wrong?" continued Lord Sage, "Your family is *gone*, perhaps, tragically, never to return. But you... you just keep carrying-on, faithfully carrying-out your duty! And when was the last time you even spoke to your own father? Do you even remember? To be blind is forgivable – but to fain blindness in order not to see? – Now that is *pitiful!*"

Lord Sage said nothing more. And Mr. Addha just looked at him, unable to reply, and slowly got out as the driver closed the door behind him. He stood there on the sidewalk, watching as they drove off to a side street next to a small park nearby.

Finally, he turned to go inside. Carrying his briefcase, he walked slowly with one hand in his pocket and his eyes toward his feet. All the people moving around him seemed to fade into a blur. Bright sunlight flashed across his path as the tall glass doors of the building opened and closed.

The Imperial Commission Court Building had a spacious crescent-shaped outer-lobby. Glass doors and high glass panels let in the bright sun. His shadow on the white marble floor faded away as he got further inside, through another set of glass doors, into an inner lobby.

Continuing down a little further, through a dark wood-panelled hall, he passed a series of double doors off to one side, just now being opened to let out a small crowd of people. An early trial had just ended. Mr. Addha stood to the side, to make room, watching as the crowd left.

There was a faint smell of smoke in the air, like that of an electrical fire. Then the smell turned to that of burned flesh. Two guards came through the doors carrying out the criminal on a stretcher: a man moaning in pain, barely conscious. His hands and feet were severely burned and blistered. He was a muscular man with long black hair, which also seemed burned and let off some whiffs of smoke. He was a brute of a man, reduced to a helpless invalid.

Mr. Addha looked down as they took him away. He moved-on and continued down the hall past several of the open double doors. He looked in, catching glimpses of the large round courtroom as he walked by. Round rows of red seats encircled a round central floor. Beyond that, there were the Judges' tall black marble desks and tall seats. And up above, there was what looked like the bottom of a great silver sphere protruding down through a round opening in the ceiling, directly over the central floor. It resembled something like a great eye looking down over the proceedings that would take place.

He continued into a small conference room at the end of the hall, put his briefcase down next to a long black marble table, and walked over to a window as he took out his mobile from his pocket and held it to his ear.

"Ben...

"...Yeah, I got your message, thanks.

"...Actually, I'm at the court building now, in one of the

conference rooms.

"...You're coming?

"...Yeah, room A-125.

"...Well, I was going to, but I was delayed. I ran into our *person of interest*... Err, actually, he found me.

"...Oh, I have no idea. Anyway, he's here, that's the important thing.

"...Huh? Wait... What? Who did you speak with?

"...Her parents? ... Really! ... Why did they call *you*?

"...Well ...I ...no ...it's not that I changed my number because of *that*.

"...Well, what did they *say*?"

Mr. Addha stood motionless as he listened carefully to every word – looking out the wide street-level window with its curved frame – watching the blurry movement outside, with eyes unfocused and distant.

Then, while he was still listening on his mobile, his eyes focused on an old man sitting outside, across the street, with a beige raincoat and white brimmed hat. Lord Sage, holding his cane, was just sitting there, on a little stone bench near the sidewalk.

He was on the edge of a little park, across the busy street with its motorcars, trams, and heavy transports. The park was full of trees and gardens, and there were some people walking by with playful children.

And in the park, near the street, there was a stone pedestal and a towering silver-coloured sculpture of a man with great wings like an eagle. The sculpture seemed to be lunging straight up into the air with his powerful wings outstretched, and in one hand he was carrying something like a long heavy spear, pointing it straight up as he flew.

The old man just sat there beneath the statue, facing the court building. His stern expression was that of silent protest. His grey eyes were fixed on the glass dome-roof of the place, while all sorts of vehicles were passing in front of him, this way and that.

It seemed like his mind was somewhere else, far away. And then, as unexpectedly as when a drifting cloud comes across and blocks the sun, he was gone – he just vanished.

〜〜〜

Mr. Addha's mobile slipped out of his hand as Ben was still speaking to him. It drifted down to the floor, bouncing under the table. He pressed his face to the window, looking franticly in every direction. Then he scrambled to the floor to pick up his mobile, and ran out through the hall, holding it to his ear.

"Ben! He's gone! He's gone!" he shouted as he ran. "...It's Lord Sage! ...He's gone!" and he put it away in his jacket. He ran down the hall into the lobby, his eyes scanning the hundreds of faces. Someone walking past him in a beige coat caught his attention. But it wasn't him.

Then he saw a white brimmed hat that just entered the front door. He squeezed through a small crowd to get closer. The person was also wearing a beige raincoat and was standing at a reception desk. So, he started running towards him. "Lord Sage?" he said, tapping him firmly on the shoulder.

But it was *not* Lord Sage. The person slowly turned around with an aged yet vibrant face. "Can I help you, Mr. Addha?"

Mr. Addha jumped back in surprise. It was that servant from the house of Lord Sage. "It's you!" he exclaimed.

The servant smiled and bowed his head slightly.

"Well, where's Lord Sage?" demanded Mr. Addha.

"I'm sorry sir, I don't know."

"Wait a minute... Why are you wearing the same hat and coat as you master?"

"I always do, sir, when I'm out of the house. He asked me to."

"What! ...Why?"

"I'm very sorry, sir, he only tells me what I need to know, when I need to know it – nothing more, nothing less."

Mr. Addha stepped back, shaking his head, blinking his eyes and biting his lower lip. He was disgusted and didn't hide it. But to him it all seemed to be a diversion, and he quickly turned and ran for the front door.

He burst onto to the sidewalk outside, looking everywhere. People were walking everywhere. Vehicles were driving everywhere. Noises were everywhere. He ran towards that little park across the street, dodging traffic.

On the other side he looked around the area where he had seen Lord Sage sitting. Everyone else in the park seemed to be at ease, undisturbed. Birds chirped in the trees behind the benches.

He looked down the street and noticed a stately, cream coloured motorcar driving away with the traffic. In a flash he started running after it down the street.

Traffic was slow for the moment. As he passed a tram, some people in it, looking out the side window, laughed at the sight of a man running faster than their tram. He ran for five long minutes, bumping pedestrians, squeezing through crowds, crossing against the signals, leaping over puddles in the streets.

Finally, he caught up to the motorcar, gasping and sweating. He grabbed the doorframe and stuck his head in the open window. "Stop!" he commanded.

But it was the wrong motorcar. Three young ladies in the backseat shrieked and screamed-out in ear-piercing fright.

"Oh! Sorry!" he gasped as he let go, and the motorcar drove off.

He stumbled over to the sidewalk with his hand on his chest and sat down on the curb, out of breath, and out of luck.

-PART 3-

A thick book sat on a table by the window in a café overlooking the harbour. "I see you've brought your 'homework'." said the young woman from the office. The young man seated next to her chuckled, as well as a second woman. Mr. Salter sat across from her as they all ate their breakfast. He had brought that heavy book along – the one Mr. Addha had given him the night before. It sat prominently on the table next to his plate.

"Um, yes... yes, I have." he said, trying not to look embarrassed.

The other man looked at the cover: *Echoes of the Aeonian Rift*. "So, Dude, why did your boss give you this huge and heavy thing to read? I mean – a *paper* book? Why didn't he just give you a normal *light leaf* instead?"

The young woman next to him chuckled and bumped him with her elbow: "Because it's a *heavy* responsibility!" The second woman added: "He probably wants him to understand the *gravity* of his assignment." And they all laughed out loud.

Mr. Salter chuckled too, but only just a little. He leafed through the book, looking for a certain page. "I was told I should brush up on some history. You know, I forgot that the Old Ryattiians – or Perfectors – not only went extinct but had spontaneously vanished from every settlement of every corner of the galaxy at the same time. It's baffling...

"I'm supposed to study one of the machines they had built, long ago, called a *gravitron*.

"Apparently it was some sort of orbital platform with a gravity engine. But its engine was more sophisticated than what we use in our star ships today. It seems that it was a precision gravity-focusing tool for lifting, building and excavating."

The others at the table looked at him, slowly nodding their heads, then they looked at each other.

"What?" asked Mr. Salter.

"Well..." answered one of them, chuckling a little, "It looks like inspector Addha knew what he was doing when he hired you!"

Mr. Salter smiled. His abilities in study were beyond question, but he craved reassurance.

"This place brings back so many memories." said one of the women, "I haven't been in this café since I worked here."

"In this café?" asked Mr. Salter, "Really? Why were you working *here*? – What I mean is, why would you have *needed* to? – weren't you an apprentice to be an *analyst*?"

"Well, it's the normal process around here. When you're old enough, you take a job in some form of service for a few years, building-up favour and credits, until you figure out what you want to do next. Then you can do some shadowing in different fields. And *then*, when you find one that's a good fit, they get you in and educate you along the way... You know, that's actually how I met Evret." she said, flashing a ring.

"Oh, you two are married. Nice! Me too." he said as he ate a muffin, "That reminds me... Inspector Addha's a really nice guy, but I really think he should get a family of his own someday. He seems so stressed out; it would do him some good..."

The others stared at Mr. Salter, a bit annoyed.

"...And that's what I told him."

"Wait! What! Oh, you didn't!" said one of the women, slamming her fork on her plate. "Dude, he just *lost* his whole family! Didn't you hear about that star liner disappearing on its way to Aerii?"

"Oh, of course." said Mr. Salter, putting his hand on his

forehead, "And Mr. Gruffly was trying to shut me up. Oh, I am so dense!"

"Well," said the young man next to him, "maybe he'll go easy on you since you've just moved here. Just don't mention it again... So, uh... where are you from, anyway?"

"Um... The arctic array. I grew up there. I got an apprenticeship and eventually became a senior engineering analyst. – It sounds like more than it really was. – I just monitored the sun's energy output, and improved ways of capturing its ion emissions to feed the e-ractors."

The others all blinked slowly in unison. "...Ok." said one of them, nodding, and smiling. "...Do you get out much, Dude?"

"Not at the array. There... um... really isn't much going on over there. Maybe that's why we feel a little pressure to have families – to make life more interesting. But actually, I *have* been going out with friends and relatives a lot more since I've moved *here*."

"Oh, you have relatives here?"

"Oh, yes, I have cousins, aunts and uncles, and grandparents are here as well. Actually, my grandfather's recommendation is part of the reason I got this job."

"Oh? Who's your grandfather?"

"Vern Rymann – my mother's father."

"Wait!" interrupted the young man, "Do you mean *Lord* Vern Rymann – as in the *Vern Rymann Aerospace Company*?"

"Yeah, that's him." said Mr. Salter as he finished his food and took a sip of some juice.

"But isn't he one of the *Founders*?" asked the young woman next to him. "Does inspector Addha know that?"

"Well, yes, he even mentioned his recommendation in my acceptance letter."

Everybody looked at each other, unsure of what this could mean. "Isn't he *investigating* the Founders?" someone whispered,

"Why would he hire the grandson of one of them?"

It was getting late, and they started getting ready to leave. Mr. Salter got up and walked over to a man behind the counter, who handed him a copper-coloured light-board.

"So, I just sign it with my finger, right?"

The man nodded – with a look of pity.

As he re-joined the group his co-worker held open the door for him as they headed out. "Didn't you have a favour system at the array?"

"Well, no, actually that place is part of the military, so everything was just provided for us."

"Cool."

"Not really. The food rations were horrible!" he said as they walked out.

"Well, remember, whatever favour you spend will take time to reimburse, so plan-out your spending." And the door swung closed.

Inside, behind the counter, a large round screen displayed a man in a suit, giving a report of recent events...

Archived News Recording

<<...More information on the data outage from last night: It seems that one of our twin-lattice stations has been destroyed. It was a communication relay station based on *Chalii* – a small rocky planetoid orbiting near our sun.

It was used to support many of the communication networks in this region of the empire, including some right here on our planet. The outage had a cascade effect that impacted a large part of last night's routine hand-off between *New Ryattii* and its counter-city, *Azimoff*, on the other side of the planet.

There is yet no word on what caused its destruction. However, three possibilities have been voiced by officials with questions of whether this was simply a horrible accident, or the latest in a string of raids carried out by *Xerquin Raiders*, or perhaps even an unprovoked attack by the *Old Forbidden Empire*.

Ryattiian forces are heading out to investigate the remains of the station. There has been no contact with any of its crew since 22_h33_m, local time last night...>>

-PART 4-

Mr. Addha found himself at a spacious street-corner, at the edge of a wide and busy traffic circle, with grass and trees, and an arched monument at the centre. The forest of buildings and towers around him seemed to coalesce for a moment into something like a symphony of organized chaos, with all the people and the relentless noise and commotion of the unending metropolis. And he began to feel himself fade away into the great cloud mass of faces. He knew he was heading for another panic attack and tried to refocus.

He looked around and took out his mobile. Then he noticed the black and blue uniform of a *sentry officer* standing at the adjacent corner with a curved shiny visor over his face. Was he watching him?

The Sentry was also wearing a discrete jet pack, which was part of his jacket. Its outer vents glowed blue for a moment. Then, like a hummingbird, he flew up silently and effortlessly to a lower ledge of a building, overlooking the intersection. Mr. Addha put away his mobile and started walking back.

After a short time, he came back into the court building's lobby. It was quiet now, as most of the courtrooms were in session. He asked someone at a reception desk for directions. At another desk he arrived and showed his identification. The person got up and walked him through a series of doorways.

In a round, darkened office a man sat behind a round desk with a curved shiny visor over his face. He sat in front of a computer terminal, monitoring hundreds of images at a time, projected onto a large, curved screen on the wall in front of him.

The man looked up through his semi-transparent visor as Mr. Addha walked in. The visor displayed Mr. Addha's information and credentials. "Good morning, Inspector Addha." said the man, "Can I help you?"

"Um...yes." he said, half smiling, "And, you are...?"

"Officer Mide." replied the man, as he shook his hand.

"Alright, Officer Mide, I need to see some recent footage of the street out front, if you please."

"Very well, sir." He didn't lift a finger, but the computer began displaying the street from various angles. "It looks like there are five sentries in the area, sir."

"Alright, focus on that small park." said Mr. Addha. The computer obeyed.

"Good. Now show me any available viewpoints of the bench under that winged sculpture... Now, go back about 30 minutes."

"Yes sir. You know, sir, you could find exactly what you're looking for if you use your own visor."

"I am aware of that, Mr. Mide, and I have my reasons. Now... there! Centre our view on that man sitting right there."

The different views all focused on Lord Sage sitting in the park. "We have footage from three sentries in that area, sir."

"Good. Now, advance at 20 times." Everything and everyone on the screen zipped around, while Lord Sage sat motionless. "Good. Good." Then suddenly he was gone.

"Wait! Stop! Go back!" The screen returned to the moment right before he disappeared.

"Alright, now... advance... slowly." A bus stopped to let off passengers, blocking one of the views. But from another angle he was able to see a black motorcar pull up and stop in front of Lord Sage.

"Who is *this*?" whispered Mr. Addha, leaning in towards the screen. Lord Sage got up, and quickly walked over to the motorcar. The rear door opened. He got in. And it drove off.

Mr. Addha's eyes narrowed as he watched. "Get me all information on that vehicle!" he ordered, "And show me where it went!"

But the screen only displayed a message...

```
             Government Vehicle: IMC-2271
        All Further Information Is Restricted
                     No Tracking Available
```

"What?" whispered Mr. Addha, "A government vehicle? What about the people inside? Can you get an ID on anyone?"

"I'm sorry, sir. There's really no clear view of anyone inside the motorcar."

"Run it back!" he ordered, "Let me see that again slowly!" His eyes were glued to the screens as he watched every detail.

"Nothing!" he said, "What about sound? Do we have any?"

"Yes, we have sound from all three sentries." replied Officer Mide. They watched the footage a few more times with garbled sounds from the street.

"Can you isolate only the sounds coming from the direction of that motorcar?"

"I can try, sir." But this time the sound went nearly silent. Only some muffled clicking from the motorcar door opening and closing could be heard.

"I'm sorry, sir. There's just no meaningful sound at all from that area..." he looked at Mr. Addha. "Are you alright, sir?" said Officer Mide.

Mr. Addha paused and thought for a moment. His face was pale. "Yes, of course. I'm fine... Thank you." And he walked out, quickly.

He went outside muttering to himself. Asking himself questions and then answering himself. He was baffled. Was Lord Sage kidnapped? Or was this an elaborate escape? But why would he use a government vehicle?

Across the street, he stopped by the bench in the park where Lord Sage had sat. He wondered if he had left a clue for him. The stone bench was unremarkable. He looked up at that silver winged statue holding the long spear. Then down again at the bench. He kneeled down and looked under it. There was nothing.

Then he got up and sat on the bench, just as Lord Sage had sat. The park was peaceful and undisturbed. The court building was directly across the busy street. He looked up at the glass dome. He could see the sunlight glistening off the silver-coloured spheres, inside, that hung over each of the larger court rooms.

Then at eye level, he noticed reflections in the glassy façade of the building – reflections of several monuments behind him. He turned around to see that it was the Founders' Broadway in the distance with its many huge monuments of iron and stone, lining both sides of the wide street.

Then he started remembering something Lord Sage said in the motorcar earlier that morning when they were riding together. In his mind he went back to that conversation...

≈≈≈

Back in the motorcar, earlier that morning they had just turned a corner as Mr. Addha closed his briefcase and tucked it behind his legs. Lord Sage was looking out his window, up at the different buildings as they turned. Then they came driving alongside a spacious green lawn and he saw the great stone and iron monuments that lined the Founders' Broadway in the distance, as they drove parallel to it.

"We never wanted those monuments." said Lord Sage, "We didn't want all of that attention on us. Too much attention on an individual is not good. Heaping the fuel of excessive praise on the flame of ego leads to nothing but trouble... We felt it would be best for each individual to focus their attention on the people as a whole – that is, what the *individual* can give to the *people*. But the *people* wanted us to have these monuments... Isn't that ironic?

"Sometimes... Sometimes, the very thing that people want is exactly what they absolutely should not have." Lord sage turned and faced Mr. Addha. "Do you know what this civilization of ours is looking for?"

"Well, I assume your question is from the point of view of a historian. So, I would say... an identity, or some notion of origin. They want to know where they're from. And I think they want to know... how they have inherited all of this." He said, pointing to the surrounding city.

"So, you would say they're looking for knowledge."

"Yes... knowledge." said Mr. Addha.

"And this knowledge, where does is it come from?"

"Well, everyone's been taught that it's from a race called the *Perfectors*." he answered.

"And where are these so-called Perfectors?"

"No one knows." he answered.

"Now, Mr. Addha, please answer this question for me: Would you rather have a bottle of wine, or a vineyard?"

"I think a vineyard would be lovely." said Mr. Addha, half smiling, "But, I don't think just anybody should have a vineyard. – If they don't know how to manage it, they could ruin it."

"Naturally. A wise answer. But you're thinking a bit further ahead than someone else would. Now, think about this: If someone had a powerful empire at his disposal, would he be so interested in a few scattered drops of knowledge, or would he not, instead, look for the source?"

"Of course, I understand, he would look for the source."

"Correct. Now, you said a vineyard in the wrong hands could get ruined. Just imagine what could happen to an entire race."

Mr. Addha scratched his head. "But you're talking about the *Perfectors*. Haven't they been gone for thousands of years?"

Lord Sage sat back and closed his eyes and sighed. "Yes, of course."

Mr. Addha rolled his head and looked out his window. "Please don't act as if that one detail had just slipped your mind." He turned to Lord Sage. "Wait, you know what happened to them, don't you? That's really what you've been up to all along, isn't it? – You haven't been hiding a few scattered drops of knowledge or technology or even history. You've been hiding an entire race – the *source*! You've been hiding the *Perfectors*!"

Lord Sage did not respond. Mr. Addha held his hand over his forehead. "This empire will *destroy* you for that! You must have *known* this would happen! But why would you *do* that? Why would you put yourself in such a dangerous situation?"

"Well, Mr. Addha, I suppose it comes down to caring." said Lord Sage as he turned to his window, "Which is something you would do well to try."

≈≈≈

The stone bench by the park was getting uncomfortable. He stopped remembering and rubbed his eyes, and his thoughts returned to the present.

In the midst of all the motion of the busy city, the great monuments of stone and iron sat peacefully above the trees across the park, behind him.

And beyond those, further out in the distance, his eyes focused on the hazy silhouette of a large suspension bridge at the far end of the Broadway.

Then he turned to the side and looked down the street towards a stairwell going down below the sidewalk, and a crowd of people going down it – going below ground. And over that stairwell was a sign.

$$= \text{METRO} =$$

- PART 5 -

Ben Gruffly sat at the conference table, looking up at a timepiece on the wall.

He sighed to himself, stressfully: "Where *are* you, Ron?" Dude Salter sat at his right, about to say something when a tall heavy gentleman walked around the table. "Perhaps a better question would be: Where is the subject of your defensive investigation?" he said as he sat down across the table. He wore a sharp jet-grey suite. His eyes were sunken deep into his round face, behind small thick round glasses.

Dude Salter stared at him with his mouth slightly open, his eyes narrow, and a look of restrained repugnance on his face.

"What's the matter, toothy?" said the man, "Ever seen a man with glasses before?"

"Um, actually... *no!*"

"Don't answer him, Dude." said Ben, as he put on his game face.

"Come on, Gruffly. What is this? Where is he? And where's Inspector Addha?"

He looked the man in the eyes and said: "Not to worry, Mr. Zoddoz. – I'm sure it's just necessary business in preparation for this hearing."

"I should certainly hope so, Mr. Gruffly!" said another man, the Judge, standing at the end of the table, having just come from a back office with two associate judges. Everyone at the table quickly stood up to acknowledge them and remained standing.

"Your honour," said Mr. Zoddoz: "The fact that the subject of this hearing is so late should be taken as a sign of contempt!"

"Mr. Zoddoz, please! Are you already chomping at the bit?" said the Judge, dismissively, "Now... Mr. Gruffly, what do you know of

Lord Sage's whereabouts?"

"I only know that he was here earlier today, your honour."

"And how do you know this?"

"I spoke with Inspector Addha on his mobile this morning, and he told me that he was here with him, sir."

"And where is Inspector Addha now?"

"I don't know where he is now, your honour. He had lost track of Lord Sage and was looking for him in the lobby, I think. But we've lost contact since then."

"I see... Well then, we'll proceed without them. Please be seated... And please close the door."

~ ~ ~

Elsewhere, down the long dark, wood-panelled hallway, past a few doors and behind some other doors, in another room (one of the larger court rooms) another proceeding had also begun.

Three Judges, wearing dark red robes, were at their stations sitting at their tall black marble desks. A number of people sat in the round rows of seats surrounding the central floor. And a few others sat behind some curved wooden desks near the centre.

"Has our next subject surrendered himself?" asked one of the judges.

"He has," answered a court officer, "subject number 3."

"Bring him forward." ordered the judge, with his voice echoing through the great round courtroom.

A slightly tall man stood up. He had slightly long grey hair tied behind his head and wore a brown sleeveless coat. He made his way slowly down the aisle towards the centre, leaving behind a beige coat and white hat at his seat along with a red ticket with the number 3, printed in gold.

Near the centre he stopped at one of the curved desks. An attendant stood behind it holding out a small copper bowl. The man hesitated, then reached in and took out two small round balls made of copper and held one in each hand.

Then he walked to the centre of the floor, also made of copper in the shape of a circle. And above, there was a huge, polished metal sphere, like a curved mirror, suspended high over his head through a wide opening in the ceiling.

He looked up and caught a reflection of himself in the sphere. And sunlight could be seen through the gap around the edge of the opening.

"Face the Judges." shouted a court officer.

He obeyed.

"Raise your arms in the air, to your sides."

He obeyed.

"Read the inscriptions at your feet."

The man looked down. His aged yet vibrant face did not reveal any expression of the fear he was feeling. His grey eyes focused on the floor near the judges' desks.

He was standing at the centre of great round seal on the floor. It was a large circle with the shape of a person in the middle, standing on the bottom edge of the circle; its head – at the centre of the circle – was wearing some sort of round hat; its arms were outstretched and curved up to about the level of its head, and there were stars around it.

And in two lines around the outer edge of the circle, there were two inscriptions. They started near the judges' desks and continued all the way around.

"Read the inscriptions, *out-loud*!" ordered the officer.

Then, with a mild tone and in a clearly educated accent, he

began reading aloud, turning around slowly on his feet as he read the inscriptions around the circle.

The 1st inscription...

> Life depends on reality. What is reality, whether perceived or not, depends on laws. And laws, whether known or unknown, depend on truth. So, it follows that life must depend on what is true.

The 2nd inscription...

> If what I say is true, then I should live. But, if what I say is untrue, then I should suffer. And if I know what is true, yet I keep saying what is untrue, then I should not live at all.

"Do you agree with what you have read?" shouted the court officer.

"...Yes, sir." he replied.

"Do you understand that you are now being placed under an oath?"

"...Yes."

"Please state your name out-loud for the court."

"...Saddir Grumman."

5

SUSPICION'S
MURKY WATERS

A man in a dark blue coat and black boots kicked up some red sand as he walked carefully across the barren, wind-swept, and other-worldly seashore, making his way towards the green waters of the surging sea. He carried in his arms the dead body of a thin hairless man with pale skin as white as pearl, wrapped loosely in a blanket that covered its face.

He stepped into the churning green waves, continuing slowly until he was almost waist-high, and gently lowered the lifeless man into the water. He stepped back and watched as the body floated for a moment. Then, just as it was about to sink, it dissolved away in the turbulent sea, like a lump of salt in a cup of sour tea.

The man stood there for a moment – his head mostly bald except for some gray hair, and his forehead wrinkled and sweaty. He raised his aged face with his pointed nose up toward the burning sun, squinting his eyes and clenching his teeth, like an old, wounded soldier who had tasted the bitter sting of defeat...

– Excerpt: The View from the Pilot's Seat
Memoires by Captain Mace Alton

⌐⌐⌐

Lights reflected off the polished steel rails above, bolted to their supports overhead, as the speeding commuter train, suspended below, glided along with a great whoosh, emerging from the darkness underground into the brilliant daylight above.

Mr. Addha sat by the window with many other people, squinting as sunlight flashed inside the train car. Steel crisscrossing supports whizzed past his window while his eyes adjusted to the light.

He was crossing part of the New Ryattiian harbour. Dozens of other parallel bridges came into view in the distance, each carrying their own heavy load of traffic, crossing the busy waterway full of ships and boats – connecting the unending city of countless glassy towers.

Mr. Addha knew how bad it all might look for him – abandoning his assignment. But if he was ever to find Lord Sage, or uncover the truth, he would have to follow his investigative instincts.

He looked at his mobile. Some text began to appear on its round screen and disappeared as he sent the message, then he turned it off and put it in his jacket pocket. But he noticed something in the other pocket, and he pulled it out. It was that old leather-bound journal he'd taken from Lord Sage's study.

"Curious." he thought to himself. He looked up, wondering how it could be that he still had it, since everything else was left behind in his briefcase.

Reflections of sunlight off of the water below danced on the ceiling of the train car above his head. The train slowed down as it came to the end of the bridge and smoothly veered off to the right, separating from the other lines, and then sped-up again. It travelled along through a half-tunnel – dark on one side, yet open and light on the other, with its overhead rails supported by steel girders. It travelled beneath a dense forest to the left, following the sunny shore of the harbour to the right. He held the journal in his hands for a moment, then opened it and resumed reading...

⌁ ⌁ ⌁

St Ives Bay, England
Saturday, April 26th, 1823

The two men trudged along on the old beaten road, under the warm morning sun, with the faithful brown dog leading the way – travelling along a grassy ledge overlooking the sea. John, with his leather brimmed hat, stepped with a quick, tireless pace, carrying his musket. And Grumman followed behind a short distance with no trouble at all – perhaps to John's chagrin.

"Mr. Kendall." said Grumman, huffing slightly.

"Yes?"

"I'm curious... I expected someone in your position would've had a horse or two."

"I did have one. It got sick and died several months ago. We... haven't yet had the funds to replace it."

As the two men continued walking, John looked out to his

right. Out there in the bay, that majestic tall ship stood waiting, chained down to its moorings. John could see it clearer now. Its massive wooden hull sparkled in the pristine waters. Its tall masts and rigging stood like three great trees on an island. It seemed to live and breathe as its crew swarmed over every surface, keeping every part of it ready.

John's heart was uneasy in him. Everything inside him was telling him that this was the Phantom, though it seemed impossible. He was waiting for an opportunity to find an explanation, but right now his priority was clear, and he tolerated no further distraction.

Grumman looked up to the left. Up on the top of a slope there were the remains of a great house. Now it sat ruined, undisturbed and silent – a lifeless pile of stones – baked and charred under the relentless sun, surrounded by the wind-swept grassy slopes.

"Mr. Kendall." said Grumman.

"Yes?"

"Those ruins to the left, some distance, at the top of the hill over there…"

"Yes? What of it?"

"It was Hamilton Sages' house. Wasn't it?"

John didn't answer.

"I'm curious. Have any of your children ever gone there – even just to play?"

John hesitated for a moment, with his head down, watching his boots – seeming to put his thoughts only into his steps. "David… has been there."

"I see… If you don't mind, I'd like to stop up there for a moment."

"No, it would slow us down too much. We need to get into town up ahead."

"That's fine. I can meet you there."

"No. That's not possible."

"But sir, I have a strong suspicion that there's a major clue to be found up there."

"I have my own suspicions Mr. Grumman. We will continue to Hayle, without delay." said John. He didn't trust Grumman at all. Besides, he thought, why would he have insisted earlier that he had never seen David, when, in fact, David had described him exactly the night before? And what was Grumman doing here now, after all these years, only to show-up precisely when David disappeared?

These questions swam around in John's head, but he wasted no time arguing. He fully intended to settle the matter, but it would only be on the path to finding David, retracing his steps exactly as he had conveyed them the night before. And so, they pressed on, down the old beaten road towards the little town of Hayle.

-PART 2-

YEARS POST RIFT: 4143+001/516: RYATTII DIFFERENTIAL
OLD FOUNDERS DISTRICT, NEW RYATTII

The men sat around the marble conference table, which was covered with papers and photographs, at the centre of the room, and surrounded by shelves of books upon countless old books full of laws, arguments and precedents.

Mr. Zoddoz had his briefcase open on the table. He brought up document after document – captivating the judge and his associates with his 'unquestionable evidence'. Mr. Gruffly sat across from him, low in his seat, slowly grinding his teeth.

"And so, your honour" said Mr. Zoddoz, "It is undeniable that Lord Sage has indeed been undermining the empire. And he surely has not acted alone. For... how is it then, that so recently, just as the empire is preparing to use this invaluable information that was brought back from his long expeditions, that it is all missing, destroyed or ruined?

"Even the so-called experts that worked on these discoveries, suddenly and without explanation, have 'forgotten' exactly what it was they were working on! It is simply outrageous! He has made fools of us all! This information could have put our empire hundreds, even thousands of years ahead of its time in capability!"

The judge turned to Mr. Gruffly. "Both of your teams have investigated this matter, Mr. Gruffly. As your chosen objective is defence, what do you have to say about this?"

"Your honour," said Mr. Gruffly, pointing to the piles of documents, "all of this has already been examined by our team and is completely circumstantial."

"Ah! Of course!" interrupted Mr. Zoddoz, "'Circumstantial' – The only defensive strategy that doesn't actually require an actual defence!"

"Enough!" said the judge.

"Your honour," calmly continued Mr. Gruffly, "all we have seen here is documentation that information was lost, destroyed or ruined. Where is the proof that Lord Sage had anything to do with it?"

"Were you sleeping, sir?" again interrupted Mr. Zoddoz, "I have shown that in case after case, Lord Sage was the last person to handle any of it. He even carefully described all of it – every single artefact, every piece of ancient technology, and every manuscript he ever recovered. He even..."

Mr. Gruffly stopped him. "Just because he's been documented as being the last person in contact with these materials, doesn't mean *he* destroyed them!"

"But, what more evidence do you *need*, old man?"

"Hey! Zoddoz!" he shouted, "News flash! When people destroy things that they're not supposed to, they usually don't document *anything*!"

"Enough! Enough!" yelled the judge. "I can see we are not exactly the kind of *gentlemen* we would like to be." He rubbed his eyes and sighed. "But... I can also see that there is evidence to place suspicion on Lord Sage, though it's not enough to be certain."

Mr. Zoddoz, with his sunken eyes behind his thick round glasses, smiled at Mr. Gruffly, who in turn looked back at him with one side of his lip raised in disgust. "Ah..." said Mr. Zoddoz, leaning back in his chair, "if one... could actually... *DROWN*... in suspicion!"

"Do you have something to add, Mr. Zoddoz?" said the judge, impatiently.

"Indeed, your honour. You see, we have only addressed the seemingly benign issue of his having embarrassed the empire. It may not be enough to convict him. Although, it certainly has *tarnished* his reputation. But there is also evidence along different lines – evidence that would most definitively *destroy* his reputation."

"Continue." said the judge.

Mr. Zoddoz took a folder of photographs out of his briefcase. And he handed out copies of one of them. It was a historical image of a newly built spacecraft and a large group of people standing around it in a hangar. The image had been taken from above, angled downwards, looking over the craft with the group of people looking up into the camera's lens.

"Mr. Gruffly, do you recognize that beautiful sleek vessel in the photograph? – It's alright, you don't have to answer. I'll tell you. That is a small *Van Rymann star yacht* being awarded to Lord Sage at the Aeonian War Memorial, almost half a century ago. Each member of the founders received one that day; and each vessel was *unique*.

"Note the elegantly swept winglets and the unusual forward placement of the engine disk. And, finally, note the red markings — Lord Sage's personal seal.

"Now, look at this." He handed them another photograph. It was a grainy image taken from far above the atmosphere and magnified; it showed a spacecraft sitting on a large area of red sand next to a round structure near the shoreline of an ocean.

"This was taken some 20 years ago by a deep-space surveillance satellite. Do you recognize that beautiful sleek vessel sitting there on the sand? That's right. It's the same one. The satellite was surveilling the second planet around the star: GR-12, of the Gorgan Cluster."

Mr. Zoddoz leaned forward, peering through his thick round glasses, and looked Mr. Gruffly in the eyes. "Do you know where that is?" he asked, "Oh, come now, I'm sure you do. It's a planet deep inside a restricted region of space — deep inside what has been called the Forbidden Empire — where any trespasser can be found guilty of breaking interstellar law."

The judge interrupted and turned to Mr. Gruffly. "Were you aware of this evidence, Mr. Gruffly? Or did Mr. Addha ever mention anything about it?"

"No, your honour. And if your honour will permit, I would like to verify that it's authentic."

"Proceed."

Mr. Gruffly handed the photograph to Mr. Salter, who was seated next to him. He looked it over and found a small round target symbol near the bottom left corner. He took out his mobile and placed it over the symbol. The mobile came to life and displayed an icon on its round screen. The photograph started glowing with moving blue lines and patterns of light beneath the surface. Then it stopped, and his mobile displayed a graph and some codes.

"It's authentic." He said, "Only standard enhancements and filters were used prior to transmission. The image has not been altered." And he handed it back to Mr. Gruffly.

"Oh, but it doesn't stop there." continued Mr. Zoddoz, "Oh, no. The law is very precise. Anyone entering in contact with the inhabitants of that region could be found guilty of jeopardizing imperial security."

He handed them another photograph, further magnified. "Look closely at that round structure, near where the star yacht is sitting. What do you see? Is it not clear enough?"

He handed them another one, yet further magnified. "Here you can see his face more clearly, even viewed from far above. Do you recognize this man? That's right; it's the great Lord Sage.

"And who is that other person? Clearly it is not human. Note the iridescent pearl-white skin. And despite the limitations of long-range photography, you can clearly see the absence of a nose or a mouth. It must be one of those repulsive Gorgan inhabitants. And so, here we have established strong evidence of contact with the inhabitants of the Forbidden Empire."

Mr. Gruffly handed these also to Mr. Salter to verify. After a brief moment he nodded. They were authentic.

"But there's more." continued Mr. Zoddoz. He handed them more photographs. "Look at these subsequent images. What do you see? Look! The Gorgan is collapsed, he's expired, with Lord Sage standing over his body.

"And look here... Lord Sage is carrying the body. Where is he taking it?

"In the next image... he is carrying it towards the sea.

"And here... he is carrying it into the murky greenish water.

"And here... he's set the body in the water, and now he just stands there, watching it float away and slowly sink, as shown in the next images.

"And here... the body is gone, and Lord Sage is walking back to his ship.

"Now, gentlemen, let's be honest. What does this look like to you? Wouldn't you say that this looks indeed like murder?"

Mr. Salter also verified these photographs and looked at Mr. Gruffly with tight lips.

"Now," continued Mr. Zoddoz, counting on his fingers, "so far, in addition to undermining our empire, we have seen evidence of illegally crossing interstellar borders, jeopardizing imperial security, and finally, yes, even murder. But, gentlemen, what do we have when all of these are combined? Such behaviour, by a New Ryattiian citizen, against this... pitiful creature, could no doubt have devastating effects on our diplomatic prospects in that region.

"Why! It could even spark an interstellar war! And how are we supposed to react to this? What should we call it? Well, gentlemen... I think we should call it... *treason!*"

〜〜〜

The judge sat back in his chair with his hand to his chin and sighed. Then he put both hands on the table as he was about to rise. "I will have to take this new evidence into consideration. Let's stop here for the day. We'll reconvene again tomorrow at 10 hours.

"And... Mr. Gruffly, please see to it that *both* Inspector Addha *and* Lord Sage are present. I don't think I need to explain to you how important it is." Then, the judge stood up, as did everyone else, and he and his associate judges left the room. One of them propped-open the door for the others to leave.

As everyone started collecting their things and began to leave, Mr. Salter looked over at Mr. Gruffly to see his reaction. He just sat there for a moment, shaking his head to himself slowly. Finally, he turned and looked up at the timepiece on the wall.

Mr. Zoddoz noticed this. "Ah, yes. How late it is!" he said as he closed his briefcase with a click and picked up a folder in his hand. He smiled and shook his head: "Mr. Gruffly, where is Lord Sage? And for that matter, where is Inspector Addha? Have you truly not been able to contact him?"

"We've already addressed that." he replied, with restraint. "Dude, let's go." And he got up and marched out of the room. And Dude Salter picked up his things and followed.

"Oh, excuse me, Mr. Salter," said Mr. Zoddoz, "would you mind verifying a few more photographs?"

"The hearing's been adjourned, sir." answered Mr. Salter.

"Ha, ha... Oh, I assure you, this is more of a personal matter."

"I'm really not interested in your personal matters, sir."

"Oh, it's not about me, lad." He said as he casually dropped the folder onto the table, spinning it so the photographs inside it slid out. They were photographs of Mr. Addha and Lord Sage seated at an outdoor café – talking, eating and then leaving.

"You see, young man, it's a question of motives. Even the great Lord Sage would've needed help erasing so much information out of existence. He would have needed someone with connections in intelligence and governmental affairs.

"Now, who do you think would have such connections, and be willing to use them?"

But Mr. Salter was not the push-over Mr. Zoddoz thought he was. And he put his hand up to stop him. He stepped up close and looked him in the eyes and said very clearly: "Mr. Zoddoz, you... are a *SNAKE!*" And he turned and walked out of the room.

Mr. Zoddoz snickered – pretending not to be taken aback – as he watched him leave the room. He bent down to pick up the photographs and his briefcase. Then he stopped. There was another briefcase on the floor next to the table.

He looked out the door and down the hall to see that everyone else each had their own briefcase – their shadowy reflections walking away, down the marble floor of the hallway, and Mr. Gruffly, leaning against the wall, checking his messages on his mobile as Mr. Salter joined him.

Mr. Zoddoz returned to the table, sat down, put his own briefcase on the floor, and picked up the other one. He put it up on the table, opened it and leafed through its folders and papers.

"Well, well, Inspector Addha," he chuckled, "it looks like you *were* here after all." Then he stopped for a moment. "What? Now, *that* is interesting." he whispered to himself.

But just then, a strong hand reached over the table and slammed the case shut with a bang. "Ah!" he screamed, a bit like a child.

The strong hand belonged to Mr. Gruffly. He grabbed the case from off the table, stood there for a moment and looked sternly at Mr. Zoddoz. "Shame on you!" he said. And he walked out, carrying both his own case and that of Mr. Addha.

Mr. Zoddoz sat there, a bit stunned, and threw his hands up and shouted-out: "Well, what kind of a man goes around with a *teacup* in his briefcase, anyway!?"

Mr. Gruffly, looking tired and annoyed, marched down the hall and met up with Mr. Salter again. Just then, two large doors opened at the side. A small crowd was coming out of what seemed to be an adjourned trial. Mr. Gruffly froze as he recognized Mr. Grumman, Lord Sage's personal assistant, who was being carried out on a stretcher, moaning in pain. His hands and feet were badly burned, and he smelled of smoke.

"We have to go. I have to check on something. And I have some urgent work for you to do." said Mr. Gruffly, as he started walking briskly towards the outer lobby.

"Where are we going?" asked Mr. Salter.

But he didn't answer. "Unbelievable!" he muttered to himself, as they marched on through the lobby with its shiny floor, and outside into the bright afternoon light.

-PART 3-

Hayle, England
Saturday, April 26th, 1823

Arriving at Hayle, John slung his musket by its strap around his shoulder and directed Mr. Grumman into a certain public house, then ordered his dog to wait by the door while they went inside.

The place was empty. There was only an old wiry-looking man behind the counter, cleaning and putting away some pots in a cupboard. He turned around on his wooden leg as he heard the two men come in.

"Ah, hello there, John." said a familiar, friendly bar tender, "Haven't seen you 'round here for quite some time, he, he! Why it's been almost a year! How are you, sir?"

"Uh, fine, Bill." he answered, walking over to the counter, "Have you seen David today?"

"Ah... no, not today, sir."

John breathed heavily for a moment. "But you did see him yesterday. Didn't you?"

"Oh, yes, sir. Yes. Oh, he's a fine hard-working lad. – If you don't mind me say'n so."

John put up his hand trying to interrupt him, but the man continued: "Ey, ey, how's that business with them copper mines work'n out for ya, sir?"

"Bill! Please!" said John, raising his voice, "David's missing. Do you have any idea where he might have gone?"

"What! Run off, has he, he, he?" he chuckled, "Oh, well, I have no idea, sir."

"It's not a laughing matter, Bill. I'm trying to retrace his steps. You're positive he was here yesterday?"

"Yes sir." said Bill, straightening his back.

"And did you see this man yesterday?" John walked over and stood by Mr. Grumman.

"No, sir. Why?"

John looked at Bill severely. "What? You're sure?"

"Uh..." Bill looked at Grumman carefully, squinting his eyes, "Positive, sir. – Never seen'm here before."

"I was told that this man came in here looking for David yesterday. Are you telling me that's not true?"

"Uh, well, I don't know, sir. I just know *I* never seen'm in here before now."

"I can't believe this." said John. "Was there no stranger in here yesterday, at all?"

"Uh, well, sir, you know, there was a man come in here want'n people to sign his paper. Yes, he was tell'n everybody how he wants to build a new road up to Saint Ives, with a stone bridge 'cross the river there. – Well, I wasn't sign'n it. I mean, sure a new road would be nice. But who's gonna pay for it? Not me! No, sir!"

"Oh, for the love of..." John slammed his hand on the counter, "Don't you understand, man? David's been kidnapped!"

Bill was stunned. "Oh... I... I mean... Oh, I'm so sorry. And here I am, rambling on and on! I'll run 'n get some help sir!" he said as he threw down his apron and put on his hat. "Judy!" he yelled out, "Judy, come downstairs. I have to go out! You haven't seen young Dave around have ya?"

John and Grumman went outside, down the doorstep, and stood there for a moment. The dog jumped to its feet awaiting his master's direction. "I can't believe this!" said John.

Old wiry Bill stumbled down the step, hobbling on his wooden leg. "I'll get some help, sir!" And he scurried into the town. John stood watching him. Then his eyes surveyed the streets and houses. He looked at the shop keepers, the women at the market, the workers on the docks, and that formidable ship anchored out in the bay.

His eyes returned to the market. He recognized someone standing with a vegetable cart. A poor older woman with grey matted hair, had caught sight of him, and their eyes locked. She recognized him. But he looked down and away.

Then he turned to Grumman. But he was looking the other way, back and up at that hill they had passed earlier. Then he turned, and his eyes met John's. John also looked up at that ruined pile of stones off in the distance. And he sighed.

"Yes, very well, Mr. Grumman. Perhaps I shouldn't doubt you so much after all. But if you have something to investigate up there, I'm afraid I cannot join you. I'll continue searching down here along the shore."

"Thank you, Mr. Kendal. I appreciate your reasonableness." said Grumman as he turned and sprinted eastward and climbed up the slope toward the high road. John watched him run off and fade away into the grassy windswept hillside. Then his eyes again focused on the ruined house far off in the distance, a charred pile of rubble, slowly being erased from the scene by all the encroaching shrubs and trees. And then he looked down and turned towards the docks. The older woman out in the market kept watching. But John never looked in her direction again.

-PART 4-

"Mother, what happened to Aunt Isabel?" asked the boy of twelve, standing in the kitchen, as his mother bent down and put some pieces of wood in the hot stove.

Mary stood up straight and looked at him, then quietly put a pot of water on top of it. "Why do you ask, Philip?"

He looked around for a minute. "I don't know. Papa seems so sad sometimes, and I guess I wonder if it's because of her."

His mother put a basket of potatoes on the table, and a smaller empty one next to it with a small knife in it. "Would you mind peeling these?"

He sat down reluctantly. "Oh, alright."

"Excuse me?"

"Oh, I mean, yes, mother."

She sat down at the table next to him, looking at the fire in the stove. Then she looked away for a moment, at the ocean through the open window. The white curtains blew lazily in the soft cool breeze. And the sound of the calm waves transported her to another time. And she sighed.

"It was before you were born. Your cousin David was very small. His parents, Uncle Hamilton and Aunt Isabel, lived in a fine house, up the road. Well... one night, while Uncle Hamilton was away out at sea... the house caught fire.

"Their housekeeper ran upstairs and saved little David. After she brought him outside, she tried to run back in for Aunt Isabel. But it was too late. She couldn't go back. And the whole house erupted into flames.

"When your Father noticed the flames in the distance, he got me up and we ran over as fast as we could. But nothing could be done. All we could do was stand there with little David and the housekeeper, watching it burn down.

"That's what makes your father so sad." She took a napkin and gently put it over her eyes. And they sat quietly at the table for a moment.

"What started the fire?" he said.

His mother sighed. "We haven't told you about all this yet because we thought you were too young.

"Your uncle Hamilton had a wicked brother named Jackson, who grew up full of greed and ambition. And he had become very bitter and jealous of your uncle's success in the navy. And as time went by, he became a wild and crazy man. And he would say crazy things. He even spoke of building his own navy and starting a war with England. – Crazy things.

"Then he started to believe that your uncle was hiding something from him. Of course, this was not true. But, gradually, he became convinced that your uncle had actually brought back a great golden treasure from some distant land. He imagined he'd been hiding it somewhere in his house.

"Well, one day he broke in and ransacked the whole place. But he didn't find anything. Your uncle caught him. But he was defiant. He started to accuse you uncle of hiding the treasure inside the walls of the house. And he swore that one day, he would find it.

"Then some time later, he waited until your uncle had left for a training mission at sea. And that night, he... just burned the whole place to the ground." As she told him the story, the boy's mother was twisting the tear-soaked cloth in her hand out of grief.

"That's horrible." said Philip, "Did anyone ever catch him?"

"No... We wondered if he might return afterwards to look for his 'hidden gold'. But he never did, and we never saw him again."

"Was he... always so jealous?" asked Philip. But his mother didn't answer. She got up and stood by the window.

Suddenly, little Caleb came running through with a toy boat in his hand. As he turned a corner he collided with his sister,

Wendy, breaking his boat. "You broke it!" exclaimed the little boy, "You broke it, Wendy! – How can I be a brave sailor if I don't have a ship? Now I'll never be a captain!"

She laughed at him, "You where the one steering it, Captain Caleb!" And the two of them ran into the other room giggling.

Mary looked at Philip. "Thank you for helping with these. Why don't you go and play with the others – I'll call you children when I'm ready for you to help me finish supper."

He smiled meekly and slowly left the table. As the children went away playing, Wendy could be heard saying: "One day I think I should like to marry a brave sailor."

~ ~ ~

Their mother stood there for a moment, again looking out through the curtains blowing in the breeze, at the ocean outside. And the sound of the calm waves transported her to still an earlier time – a time in her youth. She went into another room and opened a large wooden box and pulled out several small paintings she had made on canvas years ago when she was younger. She lingered on one painting in particular. It was a painting of several young people relaxing on the seashore.

She was a girl in her teens sitting on the sand dunes, writing in her little journal as the wind blew her hair around. Her green eyes looked up at the waves crashing on the shore. And then she closed them as she listened to the thunderous sound.

Her young friends were all around her. John was there, she called him her handsome suitor. His sister, Isabel was there, he called her his little nemesis. Hamilton was there, Isabel called him her brave sailor. And Jackson was there, watching Hamilton and Isabel whisper in each other's ears.

At one point Hamilton and John got up off the dunes and went over to the water to throw some stones into the sea. Jackson came and sat down next to Isabel and tried to whisper something in her ear. Her hand flew up and smacked him in the face. He jumped up, seeing that everyone was looking at him, and he walked away sulking.

Then, Mary lost her thought and stopped remembering. She blinked her eyes. The sound of her own children's laughter had brought her back.

-PART 5-

Distant clouds were rolling across the sky from the west. John walked carefully along the docks on the river front, near Hayle. The calmly moving water licked at the pilings around the docks as reflections of grey and blue rippled across the surface.

While his hound wandered around nearby, sniffing for David's scent, he watched the fishermen unloading their boats. Then he approached another dock with four long row boats tied to it. They were fine little boats – apparently from that great frigate moored out in the bay. There were some sailors loading supplies into them.

"Excuse me. Have you seen a young man wander by here earlier, at just about dawn?" he said. But the men shook their heads. "Have there been any visitors to your ship this morning?" Again, they shook their heads, and continued their work. "What do you call her?" he asked, pointing to the ship.

One of the sailors answered, as they all got into their boats: "She's the Phantom."

John became troubled inside himself. "Was she named in

honour of the ship that fought in the war?"

"No." replied the sailor, "She's the same one." But the other sailors in the boat stopped him from saying anything more.

John stood silently, watching as they pushed off from the docks and swiftly rowed out to their ship. He turned and continued walking along the docks. He rubbed the back of his neck. How could it be? – After all this time? He thought. Why on earth was he led to believe the Phantom had been lost at sea? If this was indeed the same ship, then what happened to its captain, his sister's husband? And what happened to his crew? Had some of these men perhaps served with him?

He turned and cupped his hands around his mouth and shouted out to the men as they rowed away: "Excuse me. Have you heard of Captain Hamilton Sage? Did you know Captain Sage?" But they were strong with their oars and had already rowed out too far. His dog came over to him, sensing that something was deeply troubling to John, and stuck close by his master.

He dropped his hands to his side. Then he took off his brimmed leather hat and rubbed his forehead with his arm. Had Grumman indeed misled him? Was David on that ship? Could his father somehow be still alive? – So many unanswered questions.

He began feeling overwhelmed with doubt. His eyes darted in every direction, and he started to jump at every sound. So, he made himself sit down calmly on one of the docks. He felt choked, as if he couldn't breathe. – So many unanswered questions; his head was *swimming* with them. And he felt as if his mind – his very being – was sinking down and drowning slowly in suspicion's murky waters.

6

ANOTHER
MAN'S DREAM

The electric humming sound increased in pitch for a few seconds, then decreased, then faded out. A soft chime rang out overhead. The polished metal door with a window slid open silently. Mr. Addha stepped out of the train onto an empty platform. The station's sign hung overhead.

=FLAGSTONE=

Outside, he found himself in a quiet neighbourhood on a hill near the harbour. He turned and walked down a street. The sun was out, but it seemed dark. Thick woods on either side of the street blocked most of the light for some distance, and the stillness and quietness filled him with an eerie feeling.

After walking about twenty minutes, he came upon a lush green lawn with luxuriant trees, like an awning draped over a green carpet. And suddenly, there it was: the great house of Sage. Only a day had passed since he had been there. Now, though, it looked different – it looked dark and lifeless...

~~~

Hayle, England
Saturday, April 26th, 1823

Mr. Grumman climbed up one last slope onto the high road to find the gutted house he had passed earlier. All that remained of that ruined house was little more than a pile of black stones and bricks, and some charred wood beams across the entrance. There was no roof and no second floor. The broken walls reached up to form jagged edges where the roof would've begun. Trees and vines were slowly crushing the remnants of that place.

Some pigeons flew up through gaping holes in the wall as Mr. Grumman stepped inside. Startled, he ducked down and watched as they flew up into the hazy sky. Then he continued – stepping cautiously over plant-covered debris, broken glass and soil mixed with ash...

~~~

Years Post Rift: 4143+001/516: Ryattii Differential
FLAGSTONE, NEW RYATTII

Mr. Addha climbed the granite steps, up to the huge wooden front door. He knocked, but no one answered. He noticed a round receptacle next to the door – a dark concave disk with a copper rim.

He took out his badge and touched the receptacle with it. The door unlocked with a click.

"Hello?" he called out as he opened the door slowly. It was quiet and dark. He touched a panel on the wall near the door, expecting lights to come on, but the lights didn't come on. A small glowing display came on instead, above the panel, showing a message that the main power was off-line.

He took out his mobile and the screen lit-up bright white. He held its light high over his head as he continued down the halls.

He came to the library where he had sat the day before. Daylight filtered in through the partially covered windows. He remembered there was an artefact Lord Sage had mentioned with concern. Perhaps there would be some explanation in one of his scientific journals. There were too many books in the library to even begin searching through. And he seemed to remember Lord Sage alluding to something in his study, not the library.

He continued into Lord Sage's study and looked around. He wasn't sure exactly what he was looking for. But he figured it would have to be either the most unusual thing or the most obscure thing that he could find.

The desk was covered with small empty boxes and pages torn out of various books. A device sat prominently in the middle of it; a model or display of some scientific theory Lord Sage had been working on.

The central piece of it was a glass ball, filled halfway with clear fluid. It was mounted in a toothed brass wheel on top of a wooden base along with some other gears – apparently for tilting the ball with precision.

Inside the glass ball, a silver wire, shaped like a spiral, was rotating slowly on a vertical axel. The spiral rotated through a faint film of light on the surface of the clear fluid. It created a blue spot of light moving in a circle on the surface of the fluid.

This little machine was certainly unusual and may have been important. But it must've something else there that had made Lord Sage so deeply troubled. It would not have been something like this sitting out in the open...

〜〜〜

Hayle, England
Saturday, April 26th, 1823 (Continued)

"John! John!" shouted an old wiry, one-legged man, panting as he hobbled down the sandy shore near the docks, "Over here, sir!"

"Yes, what is it, Bill?" There was another man following behind. John ran up to meet them both. "What is it? Have you found him?"

"No, sir." answered Bill, stopping a moment to catch his breath, "But, Mr. McDowell here might have a clue for ya."

John turned to the man. "Yes? What is it?"

"Well, sir, you see, ya know, I'm a fisherman. And ya know I keep many boats. And since it was still a bit dark when I come in, well, I didn't notice it right away, but..."

"Yes?"

"Well, sir, one of m'boats is miss'n."

"What? – A missing boat?"

"It's m'smallest one, sir – just a dingy really. I thought at first it had just washed out to sea. But then Bill here told me about your boy and... uh..."

"Oh yes," said Bill, "that reminds me, sir, as soon as I'd heard about his boat miss'n, I remembered early this morn while it was still dark, I'd seen some person climb into a small boat by the docks there and row it out in a great big hurry."

"Did you see who it was?"

"No, sir, it was too dark. But I thought it was strange."

"What do you mean?"

"Well sir, he was wearing something heavy on his head... like a... a helmet."

"Helmet? How do you know this? You just said it was too dark?"

"Yes well, even then, I could see him take *something* off his head and toss it in the boat before he'd gone. And I *heard* it hit the floor of the boat with a big thud."

John took off his glasses and rubbed his eyes. "Well, that's not very helpful, Bill. Look, was anyone else with that person?"

"No. I only saw the one person."

John slowly put his glasses back on and gazed out over the sea. He swept the horizon slowly with his eyes. And he said under his breath in astonishment: "He was alone?"

Then his eyes locked once again on that ominous ship.

ⅽⅽⅽ

Meanwhile, in the ruins up on the hill, Mr. Grumman made his way slowly through the maze of rooms and broken walls. Rotten remains of blackened wood furniture could barely be recognized in the oddly placed daylight. – A chair, a table, a piano, a bassinet.

He looked up to see a towering chimney standing, broken and crooked, atop a fireplace – a monolithic memorial hinting at the warmth that had once been enjoyed here.

He came to a charred and splintered door that led down to the cellar. It opened with a terrible squeak. He carefully climbed down to the cellar below. The stone steps were covered with ash and dust. Daylight broke in through holes in the ceiling above. He squeezed through a narrow passage that led down past racks of old broken wine bottles...

≈≈≈

After poking around Lord Sage's study for some time Mr. Addha rested – leaning against the desk with his back to it. As he leaned back on the desk he felt something with his fingers under the edge of the desk. He turned and knelt down to see what it was. There was a grove that had been worn under the edge, as if something had slid against it repeatedly for years.

He followed the grove back to a seam in a panel of the desk. There was some kind of door in the side of the desk, but no handle to pull. So, he pushed it, and it clicked and sprung out so that he could open it. The top of the door rubbed against the underside of the edge where he had found the grove.

There was a secret compartment behind the little door. Inside, he found a slim green cardboard tube. He picked it up and took off the cap. There were some papers rolled-up inside. As he took them out he could see they were very old.

He unrolled the papers on the desk. The light from the window was just enough to see that these were technical drawings – all highly detailed. They seemed to be schematics for some kind of helmet. But it was not just a helmet for protecting the head. No, it was far too sophisticated.

There were also a couple of papers that seemed to be newer, full of notes that explained the technical drawings. He turned the paper over. There was something written over the top...

> << INSPECTOR ADDHA, I believe this is something you should be aware of. But this information is dangerous and is to be guarded carefully. Some men have gone mad because of this technology. >>

Mr. Addha was bewildered. How did Lord Sage even know he would be here, reading this?

He started reading further...

> << The device was called a NUANNER PLEXUS. It used a neural network of living organisms inside and a finely tuned transceiver lining to effectively interpret the neural signals of its wearer, and it seems almost limitless in its capacity of storage.
>
> This ancient technology seems to be the key to the success of the Perfectors.
>
> With this device, not only could the Perfectors store and convey information and knowledge. By wearing it they could actually share real memories and experiences.

They did so with such efficiency that a second person, wearing it later - if inexperienced - might not even be able to distinguish these from his own knowledge and memories and experiences. »

Mr. Addha looked up. "A '*NUANNER PLEXUS*'!? ...What would one do with such a device?" he wondered "– A helmet that stores memories and experiences, and conveys them to another person who also wears it? – So that one could act with the memories of another man? And how many devices like that might be out there?"

He rolled up the loose papers and returned them to the tube, which he shoved into his inner jacket pocket. Then he started knocking over the empty boxes on the desk to see if such a device was in one of them.

But there was nothing...

⌐⌐⌐

Hayle, England
Saturday, April 26th, 1823 (Continued)

Mr. Grumman found himself in a room at the end of the passage of the cellar. Light broke in through cracks and holes in the ceiling. Soot and ash lay everywhere. A table sat in the middle of the room covered with half-burned papers. There was a work bench with some rusted tools. Charred barrels lined the wall opposite.

He was backing out to see if there was another room down there when his foot bumped into something. It was a large heavy wooden box – a trunk. He looked around for a second.

Oddly, the trunk was not covered at all with debris as everything else was. The top had been cleared off by someone recently...

～～～

Mr. Addha was sitting at Lord Sage's desk, hunched over with his hands to his head. He was about to get up. But he started looking at the floorboards under the desk and noticed a small gap.

He got up, moved the chair and got down on his hands and knees to see what it was. A wide floorboard had been cut out and then put back. He took a small blade-like tool from his pocket and pried it up.

There was a heavy round metal box hidden underneath the floorboard. He picked it up and set it on the desk. The latch squeaked open with a click. Then holding it steady with one hand, he used the other hand and got his fingers in under its lid and opened it carefully. But it was empty...

～～～

Hayle, England
Saturday, April 26th, 1823 (Continued)

Mr. Grumman knelt down on the ash-covered floor of the

cellar and opened the heavy lid of the trunk. Inside there were some old coats. He removed them to find pieces of exotic china and vases made of fine porcelain and some other vessels of copper. There was also a smaller square wooden box below. He picked it up and set it down on the table.

There was a seal on its lid. He seemed to recognize it. And he trembled slightly. He flipped open the brass latch and slowly opened the lid, hoping to find its contents intact. But it was empty. He looked up, shook his head, and said under his breath: "Oh, no..."

〜〜〜

Meanwhile, somewhere out there, in a little boat, adrift at sea, alone with the wind and the waves, David was fast asleep. The lost boy lay on his back, passed-out from exhaustion under the sun. His head rested against the wooden gunnel of the boat. He didn't even feel the hot sun on his sweaty face as he lay there, dreaming.

The little boat rocked this way and that. His hands rested on two oars, which were half-floating, limp in the water. And an old-looking metal helmet sat on the floor between his feet, rolling a little as the boat moved.

His boat rolled and bobbed in the great blue sea – far away from anything or anyone. He didn't even have the strength to open his eyes. He must've pulled and rowed all day. And now, for miles around, not a sight could be seen, not a sound could be heard, but that of the restless ebbing and surging of the ocean. And in the middle of this sea of hopelessness, a young man, unconscious even of his fate, drifted out further and further, pushed-on by another man's memory, carried-off as prey by another man's dream.

7

ANOTHER MAN'S INHERITANCE

Thunderous ocean waves crashed against the rocks in the waning afternoon light as john walked along the cliffs, with his dog following closely. He was heading up along the peninsula towards St. Ives. He looked down over the cliffs at the ocean below, seeing if anyone or anything had washed up onto the shore. Finally, he arrived at the grassy top of the peninsula. The dark stone cliffs jutted out sharply against the wind. He held up one hand to shield his face from a strong gust, as he looked out at the fishermen sailing their boats, coming and going; the barges full of minerals and ore; and that great English frigate, from a decade past, anchored out in Carbis Bay.

He took out a small pocket telescope made of brass and whale bone, and stood there, slowly and carefully scanning the horizon from side to side; and whispered under his breath. "Where are you David?"

≈≈≈

Mr. Addha looked at the empty metal box on the desk. He shook his head as he closed it shut with a squeaky bang. While he knelt down to put it back where he found it, he hadn't noticed the tall man standing in the doorway behind him.

Mr. Addha put the metal box back in the floor and replaced the floorboard. Suddenly he heard that unmistakable hissing sound of a charge pistol clicking-on, behind him.

He froze. The hairs on the back of his neck stood on end, and his arms tensed. Slowly, he stood up with his back to the man.

Then, sensing the imminent danger, he dove down to the floor behind the desk, just as the man fired his charge pistol with a sharp crackling sound. The bright white electric beam from the pistol scorched through the sleeve of his jacket and burned his arm. He yelled out as he hit the floor.

Quickly, he pulled out his own charge pistol from its holster under his jacket and clicked it on. With his head to the floor, he looked under the desk, seeing the man's feet, watching as they slowly walked around the desk. He pointed his pistol and fired, hitting both feet. The man jumped then fell, yelling-out as he clutched his feet.

Mr. Addha wasted no time running out of the study. He

slammed the door shut. Then taking his charge pistol, he electrified the doorknob until it became red hot, fusing it shut. But the other man just blew out a great hole through the wooden door with his pistol. Splinters and smoke flew everywhere.

Another shot crackled through the door, hitting Mr. Addha's pistol, destroying it. He threw it down and ran for cover, further down the hall, into the library. Seeing a door at the other end, he ran to it. But it was just a closet. He ducked behind one of the bookcases just as the man entered – limping.

He sat down quietly behind the bookcase, trying to control his breathing. He looked across the floor at one of the tall windows on the other side of the room and thought about running through it. But it was too far. He knew the man was near. He looked and felt around him for something to use as a weapon.

And suddenly, there he was, standing over him. They locked eyes for a second. In a sudden flash of white light and sharp crackling sounds, the whole library was filled with smoke and covered in shards of glass.

Mr. Addha had closed his eyes. When he opened them, he examined himself to see that he was fine. As he looked up, he saw the man in front of him collapse to the floor. And, looking across the floor, outside a now demolished window, he saw an old friendly face. And Mr. Gruffly, standing outside the window, lowered his charge pistol.

～～～

The two men stood over the intruder in the library. "Who *is* this guy?" asked Mr. Gruffly. "He looks familiar." he said. He knelt down and looked him over, looking for an I.D. But there was none.

Outside, on the steps of the house of Sage, a sentry medical officer tended to Mr. Addha's burned arm as he sat there holding his head in his hands. Mr. Gruffly was looking at his mobile, then he came over to find him. "I don't know if they can revive that guy. I wonder if he works for the Founders. We should be able to get a genetic ID on him from the database." But Mr. Addha was indifferent as he got up and put on his jacket.

They got into Mr. Gruffly's motorcar. "I... um..." Mr. Addha paused and looked down for a moment to collect his thoughts. "I found something interesting in there." he said, "But let's get out of here first. I don't want anyone with a visor seeing it." Mr. Gruffly took the controls and they pulled out and away from that place, as about a dozen sentry officers took over and secured the house. A few kilometres down the road, Mr. Gruffly pulled over to the side of the road and stopped.

"I found this thing at Lord Sage's house." said Mr. Addha, taking a small cardboard tube from an inner pocket of his jacket, and showed him the papers with the designs, "You should look it over, and have Mr. Salter look at it, too. It's something called a *nuanner plexus*. I think Lord Sage could be hiding some information with this. Try to find out if this thing could really exist, and how important of a role it could have."

Mr. Addha breathed in deeply, then cradled his face in his hands and breathed out very heavily. "I'm okay." he said quietly, "Just get me out of here, please."

RECORDING OF BENJAMIN GRUFFLY

I think Ron had reached a turning point in his life at that moment. Though, I don't think he knew it yet. And of course, it wasn't the first time that his life had ever been in danger. But I *do* think it was the first time he ever felt unsure about the worth of what he was risking.

Ron leaned against the window of the motorcar, clutching his arm and staring blankly at the trees that whizzed by. I glanced over at him a few times while driving the motorcar. But we said nothing for some time, as we raced along a span leading towards the city.

"It turns out you were right about the tea." I said, finally, "I got your message. Mr. Salter tested the sample you collected, and he just informed me there *was* something added to it."

"What was it?"

"Well, he said it was a type of neural agent, similar to the ones used to train military service-animals. It lowers or removes any resistance to commands. It would basically make someone very obedient."

"So, is that how they did it?" said Ron as he shook his head. He looked off in the distance for a moment – looking at the moon rising over the horizon.

"Did what?" I asked. But he didn't answer. "So, uh... how *is* his Lordship?" I asked with a twinge of sarcasm.

"He's gone."

"I heard you say that before, on your mobile. What happened? – Is he... dead?"

"No... I mean he just got up, got into an imperial motorcar, and... he's gone."

I leaned forward in my seat, straining to believe my ears as he continued.

"Surveillance footage wasn't much help. And for all I know, it's possible all they did was roll down the window and tell him to get in. And now, I don't know whether to consider it an escape, or a kidnapping. I don't know who to call, or who to trust. I don't know if I should chase him down, or just let him go."

"I can't believe it." I said, "He must've *known* that the system wouldn't be on his side."

"Why? What happed at the hearing?"

"Well, let's just say, wherever he's gone, he's better off if he never comes back. Mr. Zoddoz practically painted him as the worst of all criminals."

"Oh, Zoddoz! – Say no more!" he said, with a hint of disgust.

I paused for a second. "Ron, I meant to ask you: Do you have any idea what Lord Sage would have been doing on a Gorgan world?"

"No..." He scratched his head. "Isn't that part of the Forbidden Empire? When did this happen?"

"About 20 years ago, or so it seems. Zoddoz brought up what looks like footage of Lord Sage murdering a Gorgan."

"Murder?" said Ron, shaking his head slowly. "This whole case never did make any sense." he said.

"It's too bad you weren't there, Ron." I said, "Zoddoz, dominated the hearing. He made us look like children. And the judge was not pleased at all with Lord Sage's absence, or with *your* absence for that matter. They're going to treat him as a fugitive if he doesn't show up tomorrow. You need to be careful, Ron."

But he didn't answer. He focused his eyes on a neighbourhood coming up, ahead. "Um... turn off up here, please."

"I know." I said as we approached a sign that said: *Seldon Heights and Promenade.*

"You know?"

"I know you always go there when you're thinking about her."

He snickered a little, sadly.

"– which I guess would be about all the time?" I asked. But he didn't answer.

~~~

We came across a bridge and turned onto a smaller road nestled in an old neighbourhood full of small historic brick buildings and slate sidewalks. We turned again and stopped near a walkway by the water. "I'll be alright from here, Ben." He said as he got out, walked slowly over to a bench and sat down. He breathed deeply, clutching his arm from the burn.

There was a light mist in the air. Some people with umbrellas were walking with their children up and down the promenade along the water, admiring the view as a little golden sunlight peeked out through the purple clouds just before setting to the west. The glassy towers across the water reflected the colourful sky, at the same time glittering with thousands of white lights.

I eventually came and sat down next to him. He seemed relieved that I hadn't left yet. "Ben, I've been so numb to it all." he said, staring out at the ships that moved slowly through the harbour, "Even today, Lord Sage told me that I'm just 'pretending' that everything's fine after losing my family. – That I just keep on doing my duty... I don't know."

"Well," I said, "you shouldn't torture yourself, Ron. After all, Deb's the one who decided to leave."

But he shook his head. "You don't understand... I said some bad things to her. – Some *really* bad things. And then when she lost the baby..." He paused to hold back his tears. "Well, everything changed. Suddenly I realized that all those empty threats she'd made over the years weren't empty after all. She packed her things, took the kids, boarded a star liner, and headed to her parents' house on Aerii. And then..." He stopped and looked down with red watery eyes.

"What happened next wasn't you fault, Ron." I said.

"I know, but... I didn't help it much, did I?" he continued, "For the past few years I had just been drifting further and further away from her and from the children. I became more and more involved in this work, so much that I lost perspective.

"Look at me! Who works *every day* like this? – And for *what*? Look at this place! – Everybody has plenty of time to spend with the people they love. Look at all those people enjoying themselves with their families on the promenade.

"Everyone can work at what they want. Every occupation is moulded around the talents and interests of the people. Everyone is rewarded fully and equally by an empire with endless energy. And all the unwanted tasks are given to *machines* to do. Nobody *needs* to work excessively. And they certainly don't need to work *every day*! – So, what's *my* excuse?" He looked down. "I don't know what to do, Ben."

"Look... Ron... you know the world will go on, with or without you. Lord Sage will continue to get himself into trouble, with or without you. The empire will make blunder after blunder, with or without you. The entire Aeon will continue to unfold, with or without you."

"Ben... this isn't helping."

I sighed to myself and scratched my head. "What I'm trying to say is that... you have to fight to save your own peace of mind... before you can go out there, trying to save the world."

He slowly looked up. There was nothing he could say to me. He just blinked. I patted him on the back and stood up. "I know you'll do the right thing." I said, as I was about to leave. "You'll be alright getting home, then?"

"Yeah."

And so, I walked away to let him sort things out for himself. And that was the last time I saw him... before the war.

Later, I learned that a summons had been issued for him, and that later still, a warrant had been signed for his arrest for his "suspected connection" with Lord Sage's disappearance.

I don't know... Looking back, considering all the dangers he would face... I wonder if he would've actually been better-off just keeping his head buried in his work.

– The Inevitable Quest
Interviews by Danae Southendorn

-PART 2-

Hayle, England
Saturday, April 26th, 1823

Crickets chirped amongst blades of tall grass near the sea. A hand plucked some grass and gradually weaved it into a ball. Then the hand reached into a leather pouch and pulled out a slender piece of wire, shaped it into a hook, and fastened it to the ball. Then pulled out a spool of string and also tied it to the ball.

The man walking slowly through the tall grass reached down and caught a cricket and stuck it on the hook. Then he reached down and caught a few more and put them in his pouch.

The late afternoon sun dipped behind some distant clouds over the ocean beyond the Saint Ives peninsula. John came back from there, with his dog at his side. They came walking on the wet flat sandy shore, as small waves rolled in quietly from his left.

That wild black horse that had run away earlier, now came trotting along on the wet sand, circled around him and his dog, grunting and chuckling, then stopped to eat some grass by the dunes.

The dog growled and barked at the horse. But John ordered it to stop, and it obeyed. John found a pile of wood and a fire that someone had made on the sand, and he sat down to warm himself. He took out a little journal and started writing in it.

Grumman was nearby, standing knee-deep in the water with what looked like a small pouch strapped to his waste. He had a string in one hand, and with the other, he tossed a little ball and hook up into the air, swung it around in a circle over his head, and released it over the water. Then he stood waiting.

Eventually he came up with a few fish. "One of your town's people was kind enough to lend me that horse. He will be very happy to get it back." he said as he walked over and sat down.

Purple clouds sat on the horizon, blocking the setting sun. Cyan-blue waves washed onto the broad seashore of dark sand. "You knew I wouldn't find him, didn't you?" said John, referring to David, as the two men sat by the fire, eating the fish.

Grumman nodded. "He is chasing his inheritance. You will not be able to stop him."

"What are you talking about? Is it something you found, up in those ruins?"

"Unfortunately, it's what I did not find that's important. But it's difficult to explain."

"Well, you had better try!" said John, "That's my *nephew* we're talking about. I made a promise to his father that I would *protect* him. Now, I need to know where he's going, and how to bring him back!"

"Of course, I can understand that. I also have an oath to accomplish...

"What do you already know about where your brother in-law, Hamilton, went on his last voyage?"

"Nothing! Actually, until today I had understood that his ship was lost at sea. But clearly that wasn't entirely true." said John, pointing at the silhouette of the great frigate anchored out in the bay. He leaned forward over the fire and his eyes reflected the yellow flames. "You have to tell me *everything*."

Grumman looked down and sighed. And finally, he started to explain. "I'm afraid you've been misled. At the time, the Royal Navy must've thought it was necessary to conceal the truth from you."

"The truth about what?" said John, "– A lost battle? – With the French? – During a war?"

"It's not that simple, John." said Grumman, "But first you must understand what it is that they were actually concealing and why it's so valuable. – It all started with a discovery, made many generations ago…

≈≈≈

"You see, a very long time ago there was an ancestor of Hamilton, named Xavier. As a young man, Xavier had sailed on a merchant ship from England, trading for spices in India.

"One night on the way back across the Indian Ocean, they were caught in a terrible storm. The raging winds got so strong they could hardly steer the ship. Finally, the captain saw an opening and managed to turn the ship out of the storm.

"Then, all of sudden the ship just stopped. There was some sort of… *standing wave*… that blocked the ship. But it wasn't a wave at all. It was more like… an unmovable wall of water. It was so high, they couldn't see over it. It just stood there, like a great big lump in the sea.

"They tried sailing around it, but it stretched on for miles curving slightly. The captain figured it must've formed a huge circle and that eventually they would be able to sail around it. But the winds changed and pinned the merchant ship against the standing wave.

"Finally, the ship started breaking apart and the ship went down. Nine of the men, including Xavier, managed to get off and grabbed pieces of the ship to stay afloat. But the wind kept driving them up into that standing wave. It drove them so hard that they finally made it to the top of the wave and crashed down over the other side. Something knocked them unconscious.

"The next morning after the storm had past, and the sun came up, he and the others awoke to find themselves stranded on these wide flat stones, spaced a few feet apart from each other, all of them surrounded by water. As they looked around, there were thousands more of these stones spread out as far as the eye could see, to the right and to the left.

"In front of them was that mysterious standing wave. So strange, it just stood there like a solid wall, yet it was liquid water, glistening in the sun.

"And behind them there was a large island. They knew they could only hope to survive if they could find food and shelter on that island. They started moving from one flat stone to another, trying to get closer. But they found the stones closer to the island to be more pointed, and they started to slip off the stones and fall in the water.

"They started to wade through the water, but one of the men felt something brush past his legs. The water was swarming with great black eels. So, they jumped out, back onto the flat stones.

"Eventually they came to one side of the island where they found a path of flat stones leading to a tall broken gate and a dark narrow passage cut through a high solid-stone wall.

"When they emerged on the other side of the passage, they saw that this island was actually a great ring-shaped wall, surrounding a vast calm lagoon.

"At the centre of the lagoon they saw some smaller islands nestled together. From a distance they could see buildings and trees. They thought, perhaps they could find food and shelter there! But there were no more steppingstones for them to use, and there was no bridge. There was no other way, so they swam across the clear blue-green waters of the lagoon to one of the islands at the centre.

"What they found when they arrived was astonishing – an immense ancient city. The inhabitants were all gone – gone perhaps for thousands of years – but the city was completely intact. The buildings were like nothing they had ever seen. It was a lost world...

~~~

"As the days past, they marvelled at the wealth that surrounded them. There was also no shortage of food. Fruit trees and other types of vegetation were everywhere. But they soon began to realize that they were also trapped. As hard as it was to get to that place, it would be impossible to leave. And no ship could ever find them there; much less ever penetrate the outer barrier without being torn to pieces.

"And while there *were* various boats on the islands, no vessel would be able to leave the lagoon. It would be impossible to cross over the high solid stone wall or pass through its narrow passage, and over the huge standing water barrier beyond it, which surrounded the islands.

"After a few weeks, Xavier was exploring a dark vault built into a solid rock face. There he discovered what looked like a copper helmet. But it was lighter than he expected for the thickness. The inside was made of some sort of glass, and it seemed to glow like living blue-green algae.

"He put it on his head to see how it felt, when suddenly he fell into a deep sleep. He had been missing for a few days when his friends finally found him sleeping in the vault. When he woke up... he went *mad*. He ran all over the place screaming nonsense. His friends were terrified.

"After some time, he calmed down and realized that, somehow, he had come to possess the knowledge and memories of hundreds, perhaps even thousands of people, who had lived there centuries ago.

"And there were many more similar helmets in the vault where he had found this one. His friends started investigating them and trying on different ones, finding each one to be specialized to a certain field of knowledge. One of the men, after studying the glassy interiors of the helmets, poetically called them the '*dreams of glass*'.

"They had discovered a truly unique treasure of knowledge, contained within each of these fascinating devices – and the vaults were filled with them."

But John interrupted and asked: "Who were those people that lived in that place so long ago, and created these devices – these 'dreams of glass'?"

"They were called the Perfectors – the nation of Old Ryattii. They were a nation that had lived far ahead of their time. In fact, their accomplishments were far beyond *our own* time. And it had long been considered their destiny to push the frontiers of human knowledge and experience to the ends of the universe.

"At a time commonly known as prehistoric, they had already sailed the globe. When the rest of humanity was inventing the wheel, these people had been to the moon."

But John interrupted again: "Did you just say they had been to the *moon*? You can't mean that literally!"

"Oh yes, quite literally." Grumman continued, "Many of their accomplishments were beyond belief. It was a nation that had extended its borders far beyond the limits of the earth. It was an amazing place to live, and, more importantly, an amazing time. – And to those who lived there, it was the land they called *'Tomorrow'*.

"They were a lost nation, long forgotten from the pages of history. Their history – indeed their memory – was preserved only within the vaults of Old Ryattii."

"A lost nation?" said John, "What happened to them?"

"They vanished – all at once, completely, and without a trace. And our historians have never found an explanation of how or why. Only these fragile things remain – their faint reminiscences – riddles and echoes – locked up in vaults on the deserted islands of Old Ryattii – this is their legacy; these are their dreams of glass."

- PART 3 -

John shook his head in disbelief as Grumman took a moment to drink a little water, then continued: "Now, as the months past and the young men absorbed their newly found wealth of information, they realized that they had also absorbed knowledge of the key to getting out of that place.

They had learned every corner of those islands as well as every detail of their construction, including a great unseen device – a hidden machine that was responsible for that huge wall of water out there, which surrounded all of the islands.

"And they had also learned that they could control that machine. So, they took the biggest boat they could find, packed it full of food and drinkable water, oars and rigging and sailcloth, and set out into the lagoon.

"The unseen machine silently lifted the men and their boat up out of the water. They floated through the air, across the dark stone wall, across the barrier of flat white stones, and across the great wall of water that surrounded it all. And then their boat slowly and gently settled down onto the sea water beyond.

"You might have guessed, at least one of them would have needed to be wearing one of these devices to accomplish this.

"Well, they eventually sailed their little boat to the coast of Asia and trekked back towards Europe. All nine men made it home safely.

"When they finally had arrived home to England they had been gone for several years. And although many people in each of their hometowns had recognized their faces, and were glad to see them alive, they didn't feel they really knew them anymore. They had all changed.

"The men realized that what they had found was one the most valuable collections of knowledge in the world. But it was too dangerous. The knowledge seemed to be hundreds of years ahead of their own time, let alone the time of whoever had lived in that place all those ages ago. And so, they all agreed not to tell anyone about it.

"What is more, as time passed they began to fear themselves and each other. The technical knowledge they possessed was indeed frightfully advanced. As they got older, one by one, they began to disappear from the scene – vanishing from the piercing eyes of history...

≈≈≈

"Now, as generations came and went, and as fathers gradually relaxed and began to tell their children about these adventures, rumours began to circulate that some of these helmets – these dreams of glass – had been brought back from that ancient place. And a question of an inheritance began to surface.

"Soon the Royal Navy heard of it and began hunting for them, not knowing who exactly would have them. And so, a sort of silent war had begun between those hunting for them and those trying to keep them hidden.

"Hamilton knew he was an heir of this unimaginable wealth, as well as his father. And together, they used their position in the navy to keep it all hidden. One day, he finally found a number of them and tried them on. The newly found knowledge and memories that rushed into his head made him obsessed with finding the islands of Ryattii.

"At some point he must have hidden at least one of these devices in the cellar of his house. Oh, and yes, there was indeed a battle before he disappeared. He had actually pursued two French warships into the Indian Ocean. They got cornered against the very same water barrier that had stopped his ancestor, all those years ago.

"When the two warships turned to fight against Hamilton's ship, they started glowing, and spontaneously began smouldering and caught fire. Sailors jumped off as black smoke came billowing out. Then the two ships burst into flames and sank.

"Later that night, while his men were celebrating their easy victory, Hamilton slipped off into the night in a little boat and disappeared into the darkness. No one ever saw him again.

"Unfortunately, young David could not have learned about all of this before being exposed. If he has one of these devices and has tried it on, he may have had the same reaction as his father, and he is acting on the memories of a lost people and has become fixated on returning to that place as well.

"And if this is the same device his father had used, then he is also acting on the memories of his father. That's why he was able to describe me with such detail, from memory, even though he's never seen me."

John's eyes glowed from the fire in the dark as he sat there, riveted. He shook his head in such disbelief. Grumman continued: "I'm sorry, John. It will be extremely difficult to track him. By now, most likely, he will have boarded a ship somewhere and will continue to make his way from port to port until he finds a vessel headed towards the Indian Ocean. He's looking for what he believes to be his home.

"No, no, no!" interrupted John, "This morning, some people saw him jump into a little boat, and row himself out to sea! He could *die* before he reaches any port."

"Oh dear." said Grumman under his breath. "Alright. Then we absolutely have to find him. We'll sail out with the tide early tomorrow."

Grumman looked at John worriedly, "You must come with us, of course."

John thought for a moment. Then he turned his head and looked out at the silhouette of the ship anchored out in the bay. His eyes scanned the deep blue horizon beyond it. He imagined his nephew, cold and alone out there, on the vast waters, in nothing but a little boat under the stars.

Then he turned and looked over his shoulder, towards his own house, off in the distance behind him. He could just make out the little orange glow from the windows.

He'd come so close, how could he give up now? And yet, he thought, if he went with Grumman, he might be gone for weeks, or months, or even years. How could he abandon his family like that? What would happen to them while he was gone? And what if he never made it back? – Then what would happen to them? He had already lost his brother's son, so how could he allow so much risk to the rest of his family now?

He looked down at the fire. Orange embers grew bright, then

dim all over, as the wood burned hot. As he watched he was reminded of some other loses in his past. His heart was breaking inside of him. No, he could not go. He turned to Grumman and shook his head.

～～～

A large bell tolled out slowly, echoing between the towers and through the misty streets of New Ryattii. Somewhere in the cloudy forest of buildings old and new, a clock tower was announcing the time. It counted seven strokes.

Mr. Addha was sitting on a bench on the promenade by the harbour with his head buried in an old journal. He was thoroughly engrossed in his reading. Little droplets of mist fell on his head and on the pages of the journal, but he didn't seem to notice.

Then he read something that touched his heart. He stopped and looked up. He closed the little book and put it back in his jacket pocket and just sat there on the bench, as people walked by, watching the evening sky turn to night.

He stood up and walked up to the railing over the harbour and watched the sea ships humming through the dark blue waters, churning reflections of the city lights in their wakes. He starred up at the tall glassy towers as they reflected the dark blue sky and emitted sparkling light of their own. He listened to the drone of all the collective movement throughout the city. He looked up at the gleaming transports flying-off into the night sky.

There was a very distinctive vessel taking-off into the air from a small port across the water. It was an imperial Jammer. The silver-coloured warship had a sharp pointed nose. Its sleek, flat body widened out to a rounded disk at the rear. It had thin red lines from front to back. And, at the back were glowing blue vents. It lifted off with a roar. Then its engines fell silent as it sped away – up, up into the starry sky.

The world would indeed go on without him. But where was his own life going? His mobile gave several low beeps. Someone was trying to reach him. Reluctantly, he took it out of his jacket pocket and answered it...

"Yes? ...Yes this is he... I don't understand. What do you mean?" He breathed in deeply. "I see. Yes, I will, of course. Thank you for letting me know." He ended the conversation and prepared a message on the round screen of his mobile...

> Ben, I won't be coming into work tomorrow.
> I have something personal to take care of.
> – Ron

He put it away, put his hands in his pockets and walked away from the railing with just a little renewed sense of purpose. He had resolved in himself solemnly: no more. No more could he go on paying and sacrificing so much to protect another man's inheritance.

8

ACROSS THE
COLD METAL
FLOOR

*A*n older man in a raincoat walked quickly, crossing a small canal, across an iron footbridge leading to a prison buried deep inside the city. The dark stone structure with narrow windows resembled something like a giant unsightly crab, hiding in the shadows. It was an artificial island created by narrow canals that ran through the city under the streets, hidden from view generally. The dark stone walls rose from deep under the water up to several stories above. They were mostly solid, with only a few narrow-barred windows.

He came to a wrought iron door, pushed it open and came to a round desk inside. A young sentry officer, with a curved visor over his face, looked up from his computer. "Good afternoon, Inspector

Gruffly." he said.

The inspector looked at him half surprised, but he shook it off. He showed him a small document. "I believe you have a prisoner that I want to question."

The Sentry examined the document then looked over his shoulder. A figure with glowing blue eyes walked out from the shadows. But it wasn't human. It was a machine that walked as a man does – a droid. Its large mechanical body was clad in semi-transparent armour. Its silver-coloured head was shaped like a horizontal disk with two glowing blue eyes fixed to the underside of the front of the disk.

It raised its arm indicating the direction to go. Mr. Gruffly started walking and it followed. As he came to a door, another droid came and opened the door, then led him down a hall.

With one droid in front of him and the other behind, he was led along a dark hall through one iron door after another – each door opening and closing with a resonating clang. They came to an opening at the side of the hallway and turned into another that curved upwards to another section, passing in front of rows of prison cells.

Some prisoners came up to the bars to watch him pass. Their faces caught the light coming from far above. Some of the prisoners looked normal, but many were pitiful looking creatures – deformed, mutated and out of proportion. Some had tiny heads with large eyes. There was one who was pacing around his cell upside-down, walking on his hands. There was one that was rattling his bars and screaming out like a monkey. His scream echoed through the dark stone hallways.

"Can we walk a little faster?" asked Mr. Gruffly. But the droids ignored him. Finally, they came to a particular cell and stopped. He turned and looked at the prisoner inside. One of the droids unlocked the barred door and slid it sideways. Mr. Gruffly stepped inside cautiously, and the droid closed the door behind him with a resounding bang.

The prisoner was there, laying on a cot, with his back turned to him. "Excuse me, sir. May I speak with you?" said Mr. Gruffly. But the prisoner didn't move. "Excuse me, Mr. Grumman? My name is Ben Gruffly. I'd like to speak with you for a moment." He reached over and tapped him on the shoulder, but he still didn't move.

He grabbed his shoulder more firmly and pulled. The prisoner rolled over limply and fell from off the cot to the stone floor. He smelled of smoke, and his hands and feet were badly burned. "Get me some help in here, now!" he shouted.

A droid opened the bars and came inside the cramped cell. It waved its hand over the prisoner, scanning him. As the sentry came running in, he read the information from the droid's scan, shown on his visor. The droid moved out of the way as he came in and knelt down to examine the prisoner's eyes. Then he looked up and shook his head. "I'm sorry, sir. But this prisoner is dead."

Mr. Gruffly looked at him in astonishment. "– FROM WHAT?"

But the sentry didn't answer. He looked at the two droids and they came in to remove the body. Mr. Gruffly and the sentry stepped back as the droids carried him away. The sentry officer turned to Mr. Gruffly. "Unless there's something else I can help you with, I can show you the way out now, sir."

"There *is* something else you can help me with!" he said angrily.

"Yes sir?"

"You can get me a transcript from his court session!" he said, raising his voice, "And then you can get me a copy of his damned medical report!"

"Yes sir." He answered politely – almost *too* politely, "Everything you need will be available for your access in 24 hours." And he walked out accompanied by another droid.

Mr. Gruffly clinched his teeth as he stood there, absorbing what had just happened. Then he put up his hand and turned away. "I can find my own way out."

As he walked out through the old stone hallways and through the wrought iron front door, he knew something was being hidden. But he also knew it was no use fighting. And he figured the documents he wanted were probably available for the sentry officer to retrieve. But again, it was best to leave it alone at the moment. He could sense that this was a place where people could be made to disappear. A droid closed the door behind him.

After a short time, the sentry officer returned to his desk. The round computer screen came to life and obeyed the officer's thoughts. Something like a series of books appeared on the screen, moving from one side to the other. Then, all but one disappeared from the screen. It opened to a list that scrolled down. Then, all but one item disappeared from the list. The screen displayed a code. A time setting was entered.

The sentry officer adjusted his seat and leaned back as the screen went dark for a second, and part of a courtroom recording began to play...

ARCHIVED COURTROOM RECORDING

"Yes, Mr. Grumman, we know, if nothing else, we *all know* – as you have so many times stated today – that Lord Sage only tells you what you need to know when you need to know it!" shouted the examiner, slamming his hand on the wooden banister out of frustration.

He sighed as he walked back to his table wiping his forehead with a cloth, and faced the crowd seated around the court room. One of the judges leaned forward: "Is there a problem Mr. Izon?"

"Not at all, your honour." he said, and turned again to Mr. Grumman, who remained standing in the middle of the circular floor with his arms outstretched and raised about the level of his head, obediently holding up the two small copper balls that were given to him earlier.

"Perhaps we've been going about this all wrong." he continued, "Enough about Lord Sage's involvement. No doubt he's trained you to avoid detection by the metzer." Mr. Grumman glanced up at the large silver sphere suspended over his head, catching a reflection of himself.

"You've had your own share of secretive voyages. Tell us please, Mr. Grumman, where exactly you went on your most recent voyage." Mr. Grumman didn't answer. "Is it not true that around the time in question, *you* visited the ancient world of Old Ryattii – a place that is off limits?"

"I have committed no crime, sir. I have clearance to visit such a place."

"No crime!?" exclaimed Mr. Izon, "Did you not hear the opening statements? The Guardians have charged you with raiding and destroying the vaults of Old Ryattii – a crime of enormous consequence!"

"No!" he sighed, "It is true that I was there, but that was merely a coincidence."

"Then what were you *doing* there?"

"I am sorry, sir. You are not permitted to know that. And I am not permitted to tell you."

One of the judges leaned forward. "It belongs to this court to know anything that it desires. You *will* answer any and all questions put to you, Mr. Grumman."

The examiner crossed his arms as he stood there. "If you did not destroy the vaults, then again I ask you, what were you doing on Old Ryattii?"

Mr. Grumman looked down, and sighed, as if he were feeling cornered. "What I was doing was of a nature not within the scope of general understanding, sir. I was trying to protect a history."

"What is this cryptic speech? Why do you say *a* history? Isn't there just *one* history?"

"Sir," answered Mr. Grumman, "you already know the struggles that were made to rebuild our world after the disappearance of the Perfectors. This much has been recorded. But the Founders knew of something *beyond* what was recorded. I think that's why they are being hunted down even now."

Suddenly the large silver coloured sphere over his head sent a bright white bolt of electricity, with a loud snapping sound, striking one of the copper balls in his hands. He cried out briefly. And the crowd gasped.

"Look! You see? He's lying!" yelled another examiner, sitting at a desk.

The judges looked at each other, puzzled, and looked up at the silver sphere. One of them sat up and said to the examiner: "The metzer must have detected an untruth. But at this time, we don't know what it could be. Please continue the questioning."

"Mr. Grumman," continued the examiner, "are you avoiding the question by distracting the court with untruths?"

"No, sir, I am answering your question." He looked down again, sighed and shook his head. "There is... another history... that was hidden in such a way that it required discovering entirely new laws of physics to unlock it – laws that actually govern *when* something can be known and *who* may know it."

Again, the silvery sphere over his head sent out two bright white bolts, striking both his hands. He gave a short cry of pain. Everyone gasped again. The judges whispered to each other: "The metzer *is* only supposed to do this to someone who is lying, isn't it?"

But Mr. Grumman, despite his pain, continued: "These laws

were used to keep the Perfectors from ever being found. They are known as the *laws of æther.*"

Again, the metzer shocked him with a bright white bolt and a loud snapping sound. And he fell to the floor from the pain. Everyone stood up to look at him. But he got up slowly and continued: "The history you've known has not recorded what things we've seen. And you are not able to know them. If you keep insisting on going where you don't belong, everything will be lost."

The metzer again knocked him to the floor and began shocking him relentlessly, over and over, like a great and furious thundercloud in a jar, and the room began to fill with smoke. Everyone closed their eyes and turned away so they would not see what was happening to him. And they covered their ears so that they would not hear him crying out in pain.

And then it stopped. The aged man, whose presence used to be so vibrant, now lay flat on the floor, helpless, struggling just to breathe. Whiffs of smoke came off his powerless body. His eyes faded and closed as he lost consciousness, and a heavy copper ball came loose from one of his hands and rolled slowly across the cold metal floor.

9

INTO THE
CURTAINS OF
MIST

The emptiness of space falls away from you, forever.
There is no floor beneath you to support you,
There are no walls and no ceiling to hide you.
And you feel your heart fall out of your chest,

Down into the dark bottomless pit, and no longer can you see it.
Stars upon myriads of stars stand silently before you,
Like a glowing stage in a theatre full of faceless actors,
Frozen at the end of a grand and silent play.

You would lose your mind if you tried to count them all.
They stand there brightly before you, gazing at you,
Taunting you to reach out and touch them.
They watch, and they seem to know;

Even if you could swim across the great expanse,

    For an eternity, you would never reach them.

        Like millions of flowing black lace curtains,

            Embroidered with millions more sparkling diamonds,

The starry heavens muffle the sound of your voice,

    And you are speechless as you watch,

        Look! Off in the distance; a light,

            A faint light flashes in the corner of your eye.

The small dot of light moves steadily across the field of stars:

    Is it only a fading comet falling towards a distant sun?

        Or just a speck of dust floating in front of your eye?

            Keep looking. Across the void the tiny light moves.

It has form, and it has shape,

    Like a silvery leaf that's fallen from a tall tree.

        It tumbles as it falls,

            Like a bird that's been shot mid-flight.

It hurtles across the unending void,

    Powerless, as it falls towards a distant sun.

        It is a vessel – an elegant ship of the stars,

            With silver skin and gracefully swept wings,

And it tumbles through the emptiness – adrift, it tumbles.

    Slowly, it turns over – slowly, it reveals its wounds to you:

        Black burn marks and deep holes through its side.

        And it tumbles on – adrift, it tumbles on;

Falling away from you, further and further – falling;

Forever lost among the stars – forever falling;

And with it goes everything you've ever cared about.

Such are the nightmares that haunt me in my sleep.

— R. S. Addha

St. George's Channel
Sunday, April 27th, 1823

Thousands of tiny points of light floated on the black surface of the sea. Like a mirror, the calm and glassy waters reflected the dark evening sky with thousands of stars and wisps of cloud and fog. And there, on that sea of glowing starlight, drifted slowly across the quiet surface, the dark shape of a little rowboat. Its oars were limp and motionless, half-floating in the water. And on the floor of the boat, there slept a boy, exhausted.

David opened his eyes. The rising moon lit up his tired pale face. The air was still and there was no sound. He summoned his strength and lifted himself up just enough to see over the side of the boat. Every movement he made seemed too noisy in the stillness of the night. The moon was rising over the smooth black sea laced with wisps of white fog, and there was no land in sight.

He turned around to look behind him. The horizon was glowing with a dark purple colour, radiating the last remnants of light of the sunset from almost an hour ago, and he saw the black silhouettes of a group of small islands near-by. He was near the *Isles of Scilly*, several miles West of England. But his strength gave out and he fell back to sleep.

His eyes opened again sometime later. He was lying on his back, on the floor of the boat. He saw the wooden side of a large ship come alongside his boat. The calmly reflecting water sent moon-rays dancing on the timbers of the hull. But he fell back to sleep.

He awoke again but could hardly open his eyes. He heard voices around him. Some men picked him up out of the boat. He felt a stiff, coarse rope under his arms. He felt himself being pulled up along the side of the ship, over the rail, and he fell limply onto the deck.

They brought him down below. One sailor carried him down the ladder, and another led the way with a lantern. They set him down in some hay, near where they kept some animals. The sailor with the lantern also carried an old helmet that he had taken from the boat and dropped it in the hay next to David. He leaned down to look closely at him. David opened his eyes just a little. The man had a dark face and a curved nose, like someone from the Mediterranean. But David couldn't keep his eyes open. And they left him there, as he fell back to sleep...

⌁ ⌁ ⌁

Meanwhile, several miles away, on the seashore near Hayle, under the starry night sky, the two men sat by the fire on the sand. The light of the fire lit up the sandy beach. And shadows from the fire danced among the sandy mounds and crevices.

John looked up from the flames. "You said no one ever saw David's father again. But, you haven't told me if he's still alive."

Grumman looked up at John, struggling to find the words to answer him. He looked down at the fire and shook his head. "From where Hamilton has gone, he can never return." John's eyes narrowed. He concluded from those cryptic words that, indeed, his late sister's husband was dead.

"That is all I can tell you." he said, as he looked out to sea, and started to get up. "I must get back. I have to inform the captain that we'll need to leave early tomorrow, he won't have much time to ready the ship if we're to ever find David."

John watched as Grumman gathered his things and got ready to leave. "This *inheritance* you spoke of," said John, "is that what you came here for – to give to him?"

Grumman stood up and put his sack of things over his shoulder. "If you had asked me that same question a few years ago, I might have said *yes*. I was a stubborn man then, with my own ideas. I wanted to rebuild that which those Ryattiians had left behind and put their memories to useful work. And there were many others who shared my point of view. But we had underestimated the risks.

"Those devices were meant for a people much more advanced than us, as tools for conveying knowledge quickly and efficiently. But they're too dangerous. If these things fell into the hands of people of this world and of this period, they could destroy themselves and everyone else along with them."

John scratched his head slightly and stood up also. "Well, if you didn't come to give David this inheritance, why *did* you come?"

"I came to put an *end* to it." he said, "I intended to *eliminate* any trace of those machines before anyone had ever found them. Unfortunately, David *did* find one of them, and is now relentlessly pursuing another people's inheritance. But he should not pursue it. And I fully intend to find him before any harm comes to him.

"John," said Grumman, with his hand firmly on his shoulder, "I will do everything I possibly can, to bring him back to you."

"Well," said John, after holding back a tear, "what should I do if I happen to find *more* of these devices – these dreams of glass?"

"Smash them! Burn them!" answered Grumman, as he kicked sand over the fire, snuffing it out in a cloud of white smoke and steam. "The dreams of glass must be destroyed!"

John looked on as the man got up onto that black horse that was obediently waiting nearby. And Grumman turned and looked back at John. – His aged yet vibrant face now lit only by the bright moon.

"And what's more," he added as he tossed a small sack of gold coins to John, "I think you should buy yourself a horse to replace the one that died." Then he rode off, towards Hayle, and he disappeared into the night.

John stood alone with his dog standing at his feet, by the smothered fire, as the glowing embers died down and white smoke blew out over the black sea, in the soft breeze...

≈≈≈

The dark stone house perched like an owl on the ridge overlooking the sea. As John came in from his long walk back across the moon-lit dunes, Mary met him at the door. The children were asleep on the floor, wrapped in blankets by the warm fireplace. His dog also came in and laid down next to them. They had fallen asleep waiting for him to return with their lost cousin. He looked at Mary and shook his head.

The two of them sipped some wine, as they sat in wingback chairs across from the children, watching as they slept. John quietly explained to her everything that had happened. "I trust Grumman to do what he said. But I only trust him because I have no choice. He was the only source of answers, and now... he's the only person who seems capable of finding David.

"Incredible as it was to hear all his stories," continued John, "I still felt as though there was something important he *wasn't* telling me. But I couldn't even formulate the questions. And he was very careful not to spark any confrontation between us."

Mary shook her head. "And what are we supposed to do now?" she said, "Is our family just going to keep being strung along by the faint hope that this man might actually bring David home?" But she didn't wait for an answer. She stood up quietly, wrapped herself in her shawl, and went upstairs.

John remained. He took his glass of wine from a little table beside his chair, and just sat there quietly. As he sipped his wine, he looked at the children sleeping on blankets by the glowing fireplace. He took off his glasses and put them on the little table, and slowly cradled his head in his hand.

-PART 2-

Down in the dark, below deck, the creaking sound of the ship resonated through all its heavy timbers. Two Turkish sailors stood over David. One of them, holding a lantern, kneeled down and nudged him to wake him up. His eyes opened slowly, and he struggled to sit up in the hay, below deck, near the animals. "Where did you come from?" asked the sailor. But he didn't answer. "This English boy and his boat came out of the middle of the sea." said the man to the other, as he stood again. "I saw no other ships. Did he row all the way from England?"

David sat there quietly, clutching his aching arms. "He looks so weak and sickly." said the other man, "Maybe his ship sank."

A third man came in. He was not like the others. His skin was lighter. He had a thin beard and streaks of grey hair mixed with black.

"Stand up for the captain!" said one of the sailors, lifting the boy to his feet. But he stumbled back down into the hay. "It's alright." said the man, with an English accent, "What's your name, lad?"

"Uh, I am David Sage." he said as he sat up and pulled himself up against the timbers.

The man kneeled down in the hay. "Sage?" he said, looking him in the eyes, "And what is your father's name?"

The boy hesitated. "Hamilton Sage."

The man looked stunned and examined the boy's face more closely. "I can't believe it! You're Hamilton's boy? Did you actually row that tiny boat all the way from Gwithian?"

David kept his distance. He seemed to recognize the man and was visibly fearful. "There's no need to fear me, young man." he said with a grin, "– Though, you probably wouldn't remember me. I am your uncle. I am your father's brother." And he stretched out his hand to shake his. "My name is Jackson Sage."

But David didn't shake his hand. "Yes, I know who you are." he said.

The man took back his hand. "You do?" he said, as his smile turned to a frown, "How could you? I only saw you when you were a baby." He glanced down at the floor. Something caught his eye near David's feet. He reached over and picked up an old looking helmet and dusted off some of the hay from it. "Ah!" he said quietly, "Is this what I think it is?"

The helmet was dull copper in colour. He held it firmly, feeling the ancient metallic casing. It was very rigid. But it was not actually metal at all. It had the porous organic texture of bone or shell.

He turned it over and looked at the inside. "Look how it glows!" he said. The glassy interior shimmered and glowed with a blue-green organic light that moved about beneath the surface.

"So," he said, his brown eyes glancing up at David, "is it possible that you know who I am because you've inherited your father's memories? What else have you received from this device? What other treasures lay inside it?"

The glowing light from the glassy interior captivated his eyes. "I've only heard the whispered rumours of old men on their deathbeds – stories of an inheritance of treasure unlike anything in this world. I've only heard the confounding riddles of crazy drunkards in the streets at night – stories of living memories from a kingdom of long ago.

"At last, I can hold it in my own hands! But could I dare to wear it on my own head?" And slowly he lifted it over his head, and he put it on. But the man screamed out in pain and fell to the floor. And he threw the helmet down. "What is this!" he shouted, "Can this thing actually reject me?"

The other two sailors helped him back to his feet. "Alright." he said, as he straightened his hair and fixed his shirt collar. "We had not planned to stumble upon this discovery. I need some time to think." He picked up the helmet and marched out, taking the lantern with him. "Give him some water and something to eat!" he ordered as he left.

They obeyed and eventually left David there in the dark alone. His eyes slowly adjusted as some silver moonlight pierced the darkness in the ship, through the wooden gratings and hatches above his head.

His grey eyes fixated on the dusty white moon beams that filtered in. Tired as he was, now he could not sleep at all. His head was buzzing with questions upon questions. But as time passed, he realized that he already had many of the answers, mysteriously implanted in his mind.

Not only that, but he started to understand the device itself, realizing that he somehow possessed the memories of the ancient people who created it.

He realized that the device was not just a container of memories. And it was more than just a conveyor of knowledge. It actually seemed to have a sort of intelligence, and an awareness of who was wearing it. And it could choose what knowledge to reveal and to whom to reveal it. It actually seemed to be alive. Indeed, some of the material from which it was made truly was living material. But more than that, he realised that it was actually a living mind.

Elsewhere in the ship the pale faced man in his dark cabin sat at his desk. He held the helmet in his hands, resting it upside down under a lamp on the desk. The glassy interior glowed with moving organic blue-green light.

What would a man do with such a thing? Somehow he knew he could never wear it, again. – It had rejected him. So, was it useless to him? The knowledge contained in it was far too valuable to throw away.

At the same time, alone in the darkness, David thought with the wisdom of countless generations. What would a man do with such a thing? He realized he was not the first to ask this question. And he came to the same conclusion as had an entire nation, long ago.

A man would desire the power that such knowledge could give him. And once he tasted it, he would do anything to get it. And if he could not get it, he would try to control those who already had it. And if he could not control those who already had it, he would come to fear them, and he would try to kill them.

≈≈≈

YEARS POST RIFT: 4143+002/516: RYATTII DIFFERENTIAL
THE LANDINGS, NEW RYATTII

Just a few minutes past midnight, down on the ground below,

the dim orange streetlamps resembled a sort of upside-down sky with stars set into a rigid pattern.

A black rip-wing hovered quietly over the sleeping neighbourhood. It looked like a giant dragon fly with four wings. Each wing had a glowing blue engine near the tip. Four sentry officers jumped out and floated silently down towards a building. Their discrete jetpacks let out blue streaks of light from their backs. And their black uniforms masked their shape against the hazy night sky.

They descended onto the terrace of a building and walked up to a sliding glass door. The apartment was dark inside. One of them took his badge and touched it to a curved receptacle next to the door. The door clicked, and he pulled it open.

"Inspector Addha?" called out the man. But there was no answer. The men all took out their weapons and walked into the dark apartment. Patches of fabric on their uniforms began glowing brightly, lighting up the place.

They searched both floors, room by room, under beds, and through all the closets. But they found no one. The apartment was empty...

〜〜〜

Elsewhere, underground, in a central train terminal, a man in a worn-out suite jacket stood on a quiet platform with a small suitcase on wheels by his side. He stood for a moment in front of a machine attached to the wall and touched a few symbols on its round screen. It dispensed a ticket for him, and he looked at it in his hand.

He looked up at a timepiece hanging from a shiny copper ceiling. It was made in a classical style. It read half-past-midnight.

A warm breeze blew in from the tunnel at the end of the platform with a howling sound. And after a few moments a heavy monorail train emerged, whooshing into the station. The sleek silver train gradually slowed down. Its jagged nose with three large headlights pulled smoothly into the station. It made a low humming sound that increased in pitch as it slowed, then faded out as the train came to a smooth stop.

When it opened its doors, the man in the worn-out suit, pulling his little suitcase, walked over to the train and waited as a few sleepy people got off. Then he got on.

He put his suitcase under his seat and sat down. After a few minutes, the train closed its doors and made a high-pitched humming sound as it started moving. The sound deepened then faded out as it picked up speed, whooshing out of the station.

~~~

St. Agnes, England
Sunday, April 27th, 1823

The hazy blue light of dawn trickled into the dark ship. David awoke, lying in the hay. The men on the ship where rushing this way and that, getting the ship ready. As he got up he could see them more clearly. These were rough looking men. They looked like criminals.

He stood up slowly and walked calmly to the ladder. He went above deck and stood at the bow, watching as they raised anchor. He looked around at the ship and realized that these men were actually pirates.

Through all the clamour and commotion of the men, he saw the tall pale faced man – who claimed to be his father's brother – standing at the back of the ship, looking right back at him. The man turned to one of his crew members and spoke in his ear.

"Mr. Ahmed, did I ever tell you about the time my brother lost his mind?"

The other man shook his head. "No? Surely, I've told about him! He started to believe he was from a place called *Ryattii*. I *have* told you about the legends of that place. – About the unimaginable treasures hidden there. And how no one knows where it is.

"Well, *my brother* knew, but he kept it secret. He started to believe it was his home, and he stopped at nothing to go back. I believe his boy also has this madness. – And he may also believe that Ryattii is his home.

"Unfortunately, it seems he's also inherited his father's distrust of me... So, I want you to take the wheel, Ahmed, and place the boy at your side. Tell him we will take the ship to wherever he calls home.

"Keep me informed of our direction. His uncle's house is in Gwithian, east from here. So, if he takes us east, then he does not have this madness. And we can dispose of him.

"But, if he requests any direction other than east, then he must also believe he is a Ryattiian. He will lead us straight to that legendary place. And we will be among the richest men on Earth."

He went down to his cabin. The other man pointed to David and shouted with a crackled voice: "You there! Boy! Come here!" David reluctantly obeyed. The crew paused their activities for a moment to let him through as he walked across the deck. "Come with me." He took him over to the ships wheel and said to him: "The breeze is picking up. To where shall we set sail now?"

David looked confused. "Why are you asking me?"

"Because the captain said that, as a favour to his nephew, it would be our pleasure to take you to wherever you call home. Now, tell me, which way should we go?"

The boy looked around to get his bearings. Wisps of mist drifted by the ship. The morning breeze blew his hair a little as he turned his head.

Finally, he pointed, and he said: "We should head *south*." The man's eyes widened. "Very well." he said as he grasped the wooden ship's wheel. "Mr. Berk," he said to another crewman, "– please inform the captain – we shall be heading *south*." The man nodded and walked away, as the others worked quickly to unfurl the large brown sails…

≈≈≈

Several miles away, in Gwithian, small ripples in the calm ocean water dabbled quietly on the English seashore. The dark stone house perched like an owl on the ridge overlooking the sea, wrapped in a blanket of white fog. John stepped out into the morning mist. The ground was damp with dew. He walked down to the sandy strand to watch the Phantom set off in search of David.

He could just see the great English warship sitting in the fog, glistening in the first rays of the sunrise, and a less-than-full-moon setting behind it.

He felt a little tug at his side, and he looked down. Little Caleb had come out to join him. "Will they bring our Dave home, papa?"

"Yes" he replied, half-smiling, "Yes, they must." And he stood there, with one hand on his little boy's head, watching.

In the dead quiet of the early morning, they could just barely hear, echoing from across the glassy water, the whistles and calls of the officers as they spurred-on the crewmen to ready the ship.

Its anchor was raised out of the water, splashing water from the heavy chains. Its white sails were unfurled and let loose from their lashings. They filled and puffed out with the light air as wisps of morning mist drifted past. And the distinctive British long red pennant waved slowly from the highest point on the tallest mast.

"Go on!" said John, under his breath, as Caleb looked up at him, "Go on, you Phantom! Find our little boy. Bring back our David home!"

-PART 3-

YEARS POST RIFT: 4143+002/516: RYATTII DIFFERENTIAL
NORTHWEST CORRIDOR, GREATER NEW RYATTII

The silver train sped across the green dew-covered valley. It glided smoothly on its monorail-track with a whoosh, barrelled through dark wooded areas, and launched across bridges, over rivers and ravines in the cool blue light of dawn.

Many of its passengers were asleep as the countryside and rolling hills flew past their windows. One man, though, was not asleep: a young man in an old worn-out suite jacket – as my friends would often describe me. Though, I never really thought of myself as a young man. I felt old.

I couldn't read that little old journal anymore, and I put it away in my suitcase. The only thing of relevance in it was the name of Sage, and a collection of devices called dreams of glass, that resembled the nuanner plexus Lord Sage had mentioned in his notes.

I had felt a connection with that journal, though. I think it resonated with me because of some similarities with struggles that I had had in my own life.

I leaned against the window with my fist to my nose and just stared out at all the greenery laced with fog, whizzing past my window. But my eyes couldn't focus. My life was taking a turn, and I didn't know where it was going. And I tried to take-stock of what there was of value left in my life.

Some time ago, my former therapist – now a reporter and author – once recommended that I write my own journal to help me, and that I add an entry whenever I was having trouble coping. I regret to say that this is one of *many* entries in that journal. – And to anyone unfortunate enough to be reading it – my sincere apologies.

Death was never something we were accustomed to in our world. – No more so than sickness, or poor health due to age.

Sure, we had our doctors who loved to study the elegant structures and systems of the human body. But it was only for the purpose of either healing those who had had an accident, or for advancing our own knowledge and finding new and better ways to apply designs found in nature.

Here, people didn't use the words *life span*, unless they were discussing plants or animals. Until recently it was unheard-of for someone to die simply because they had reached a certain age. Most people have been alive for hundreds and even thousands of years. The Founders are among the oldest people of our world – some having lived for at least 5 thousand years.

It is only recently that people have started showing signs of advancing age. Indeed, many of the founders have died by now, as well as many others not nearly as old as they are.

Of course, we knew that death was common on other worlds, far away, but not *here*. *Here* it was always something rare for us, and as a people we never really learned to cope with it. – At least I never did.

~~~

I stood for a moment admiring the picturesque view from the front lawn. The grand brick house sat prominently on the side of a hill overlooking a river valley. Its porch wrapped around it with classical arches. Inside, the house was filled with things of comfort: soft sofas and chairs, bright open windows. It was also filled with historic and collectable items: paintings, musical instruments and artefacts. – Sound familiar?

"Mr. Addha, welcome!" said a distinguished, though humble looking man. "And may I say, thank you for responding so promptly."

"Thank you, Doctor Bushbeck. It was good of you to call me."

"Here, let me take your coat and suitcase upstairs." he said, as I took off my jacket, "And while you are staying, would you prefer a bedroom facing the valley or the sunrise?"

"Oh, the vall... I mean... Um... the sunrise, please."

"Of course, sir."

He raised his arm in the direction of the sitting room. "If you please, sir, your father is right in there. He's far too weak to walk, so we moved his bed into the sitting room. He wanted to be – as he put it – where the life of the house is."

My eyes couldn't blink as he left me there. I walked slowly across the warm coloured hardwood floor, through the bright open hallway. At the end of the hall, white curtains blew in the soft morning breeze coming through the large open windows in the sitting room. Some young women in long white dresses walked through with nursing supplies. One also brought over some tea and set it down on a small table next to a bed.

I cleared my throat a little.

"Oh... I think you have a visitor, Professor Addha." said one of them.

Covered in the white sheets of his bed, and comfortably resting in his robe and nightclothes, the man sat up slowly in his bed and looked at me. He was pale and wrinkled. His once full dark beard now was thin and grey. But his vivid green eyes gazed at me with the same intensity as before.

"You look horrible!" he said, as he laid back down.

I took a step back, not quite believing that *he* was actually saying *that* to *me*. "I beg your pardon?" I said smiling, "How are you Dad?"

"Well, better than you, I should say! What's happened to you? You're all worn-out!"

"Well, I've been working." I said with a shrug.

"Of course." he said, rolling his eyes.

A nurse poured his tea from a fine white porcelain teapot. "Would you also like some tea sir?" she said to me.

"Thank you, miss, no." I said appreciatively, as I pulled over a chair and sat down. Then she walked away quietly.

A silent moment set in. I looked around from my seat, feeling a bit uncomfortable. It all seemed a bit reminiscent of another visit I had had with another older gentleman only a day and a half earlier.

"Oh, by the way" I said, to break the ice, "Ben and Margie send you their greetings."

"Ah!" he said smiling, "Those two have been dear friends of mine for a long time, and um, they've been great admirers of you as well.

"You know, when we were younger, we had helped each other through many difficult situations; and we made many lasting memories in the process. There were even some very dangerous missions Ben and I had been on, including some flying with Captain Mace's squadron. That was many, many years back. But I've told you those stories already – a lot of stories – and our families have been very close ever since." He looked off into the distance, lingering in the nostalgia. "Well, anyway, how long are staying with us?"

"Uh, I'm not sure – a few days."

"Well, take anything you want while you're here. Oh, and there's a jacket I'd like to give you."

"Is it the brown leather one?"

"That's the one! Hehe! – But I want my other one back if you please. That one was a loaner after all. – And no doubt it'll need a trip to the tailor's."

"Yes sir!" I said, smirking.

Then he looked at me with a serious face. "How have you been coping, son?"

I looked down. "I can't say I *have* been coping, really. – Just staying busy, working hard."

He leaned over on his elbow, looking towards the window, and slowly put his fist to his nose. "You know, when your mother slipped away, I had to work hard as well. But my work was to avoid slipping away *myself* – into an emotional coma. And it was to make sure that you and the others really truly felt... *alive.*

"You have to fight, Ronald. You must... *fight.*"

I half smiled. "Hmm... Ben said something like that to me, just yesterday. He told me... I have to fight to find my own peace of mind." I said, scratching my head, "But... my mind is a war zone. Where do I even *begin*?"

"Well," he said quietly, straightening the sheets of his bed, "...have you spoken with her parents?"

"Her parents? ...No."

He leaned forward on his bed, looking into my eyes. "Well..., you can begin *there*."

I started staring off into the distance. He looked at me, shaking his head. "Good grief!" he said, "You really *do* look terrible!" And we laughed at the irony of the moment.

〜〜〜

Upstairs, alone, I unpacked a few things in my guestroom and looked around. There were a lot of things brought over from my old house where I grew up. There were even some old pictures of me as a child with my siblings. It made the room feel very familiar. The doctor knocked softly. He had brought the brown leather jacket my father wanted me to have. "Thanks." I said.

"The housekeeper has some dinner prepared for you." He replied before leaving quietly. I put the jacket on the bed next to my things and picked up mine – err – the loaner and brought it down to my father.

"Good grief! Come on!" he shouted, as he examined the scorched and tattered sleeve. "What have you done to it!?"

A little later, after eating something, I wandered around the rooms and hallways looking at my father's collections. He was the influence that had led me to appreciate history in my early years. He had collected all sorts of fascinating treasures, from every corner of the empire.

The place was like a museum. Across the sitting room, where my father was, there were even large display cases with actual metal suits-of-armour.

There was a plaque next to one of the displays that read...

> *A*rmour used in the War of
> the Great Aeonian Rift.
> – *Circa 100* Y.P.R.

There were also some ancient silver coloured charge pistols and charge riffles, with other devices and tools displayed beside them. I noticed another plaque which read...

> The warriors of the old Ryattiian Empire were not feared so much for their might, as much as they were feared for their knowledge.
>
> Battles were won, not by over-powering their enemies, but by trapping them in their own ignorance.

I walked through the sitting room, looking up at the displays. My father noticed me walking by slowly. I looked at him. He seemed very tired. "I see you still haven't lost your love of history." I said.

"Of course, history is the reason things are the way they are." he said.

"And how do you like this new house of yours?"

"Well, it's a good fit." he said with a cough.

"Indeed. And what about this little town, Angel's Lance? – It doesn't exactly strike me as a 'good fit' for you. – I mean, it doesn't seem very *historic*, does it?"

"Funny you should say that." he answered, "That's actually part of why I chose to move here." he said with a cough. He paused to catch his breath. "At least, I should say, before I became so terribly ill."

I looked away, not wanting to stare at his discomfort, and I continued walking slowly, looking up at his displays. "For example," he continued, "do you know why this town is actually called Angel's Lance?"

"Not at all." I said, seeing my own reflection in the glass display cases.

He touched his finger to his nose and turned toward the windows. "Well, as the legend goes, thousands of years ago, some people living in this place saw something frightful falling from the sky. From the descriptions I've compiled, it must have been huge. It would have resembled one of our great modern-day centroids. It was long and slender. It fell from the sky in a roar of thunder and burst into flames as it shattered against the mountains into a million pieces. And all those pieces scattered throughout the valley below.

"Well, the people that lived here screamed in fear and ran for their lives. And they spread the story wherever they went. And from then on, whenever they spoke of this place, they called it the valley of the *angel's lance*."

As he told me the story, I remembered seeing Lord Sage the day before, sitting under that statue of a winged man carrying a spear. I wondered if he had actually been trying to tell me something.

"So..." he said with a cough, "as everyone should know, history is the reason things are the way they are."

I was walking around looking at the displays, still listening as he finished. But I noticed something on one of those suits-of-armour, inside one of the display cases. – A round symbol on the breastplate. I started walking towards it.

The symbol looked very familiar. It was a large circle with a person in the middle, standing on the bottom edge of the circle; its head, with a round hat at the centre of the circle; and its arms outstretched and curved up to the level of its head; and there were stars over its head.

It reminded me of a description of a drawing in that old journal. I thought about comparing it, but at the moment I couldn't quite remember where I had put it.

"You left something in your coat pocket, Ron."

"What?" I said, glancing over my shoulder. He was holding the journal in his hand. "Oh, there it is." I mumbled.

"I hope you don't mind, but I read some of it." he continued, "And, oddly, I feel like I've read it before. – It's beautiful. Let me see. There's a part I especially like..."

He looked carefully through the book, as if it were one of his artifacts. Thinking back to that day – how so much of what he said just failed to register with me – it was, sadly, all too typical of me.

"Ah yes, here it is..." he continued, and began reading...

> *Once upon a rainy morn' on the windy shores of England, a tall and slender navy-man bid his son farewell.*

My attention, though, was fixated on the display in front of me. I examined that symbol again on the breastplate. – The figure wearing that round hat. Could that be the *device* that Lord Sage was referring to? I looked up at the other pieces of armour: the arm plates, the chainmail, the shoulder plates, a facemask and its semi-transparent visor. And displayed above all this was a large decorative silver helmet. – Really it was just an outer shell. And beneath the silver helmet: a copper-coloured inner helmet.

I stared at it in disbelief. The under-part of that inner-helmet seemed to be glowing with an organic blue-green light. My eyes opened wide, captivated by the glow. I couldn't believe it. I had found it! I had actually found a *nuanner plexus* – that ancient reminiscence device – one of those legendary *dreams of glass*!

> *"Will I never see you again, Papa?" sobbed the little one of four.*

"Hey, Dad!" I shouted, "Where did you get this!? And how long have you had it!?" I laughed. I was ecstatic! I couldn't stop admiring its beautiful, other-worldly appearance.

So captivated was I, however, that I didn't notice the clamour of feet against the hardwood floors behind me. Neither did I understand the hurried and frantic words spoken among the people behind me.

> *"Oh, keep me in your heart and do not forget me, and I will be with you forevermore." said the man, kneeling, with one hand on his little boy's little heart, and with the other, wiping away his little tears. "I will always love you, my son."*

Finally, I turned my head. The doctor and all the nurses were standing around my father's bed, trying to revive him. Someone bumped into the little table next to his bed and knocked it over. The white porcelain teapot and the little cup of tea floated down to the floor and shattered in a strange slow and silent crash.

> *Then once after a long embrace the sad sojourner embarked.*

Just as suddenly as that, the last precious part of my life fell away from me, into an endless void. I stood still, frozen, unable to recognize the faces coming over to me, to comfort and console me. And just as suddenly as that, my mind filled with memories and pangs of guilt. – All those invitations that I had declined, all those conversations I had avoided. – It was never meant to disrespect him or downplay his role in my life.

And slowly, so ever slowly...

He had said that I was highly admired. But if history is indeed the reason that things are the way they are, then he was the reason that I am who I am.

...the tall ship with her tall captain...

I stared out through the white curtains blowing in the cool breeze, out through the window at the clouds of fog draped delicately over the tree-covered hills. They became in my eyes as great waves and surges in the ocean.

...slipped away quietly...

And the flood of loss and guilt broke through its gates and swept me off into an endless sea – never to return – drifting forever...

...into the curtains of mist.

10

DAVID SAGE

The early morning dew fell through the leaves in the forest with a muted pitter-patter. The hazy blue light filtered in through the dark wet tree branches. A long-feathered cuckoo flew onto a branch, knocking off some drops of water from the leaves, and its eerie call echoed out through the trees. And in the mud, down below, some boot tracks collected the water of the falling dew.

The green foliage along the forest floor seemed to glow with fresh radiant life. A hand wearing a black glove gently pushed aside some fern leaves close to the ground and a man with a scope peered through. On a lush green hill across a small river, the classical brick house sat quietly in the morning fog. He looked down. Other men in black uniforms stealthily made their way down the slope towards the river and vanished into the fog that cloaked both sides.

Inside the house it was dark and still. Then, with a bang and a smash, the door was kicked in. A little ball was thrown in. It rolled a short distance then exploded in flash and a cloud of smoke.

A dozen soldiers in black uniforms, with breathing masks under their round transparent visors, and carrying charge rifles in their hands, burst into the house. Screams were heard as they went room by room, grabbing everyone they found as they identified them with their visors – the nurses, the servants, and finally the doctor, who demanded an explanation. But nobody gave him one.

They tied their hands and took them outside to sit down on the wet grass. At the same time three large rip-wings roared in overhead and landed most irreverently on the lawn. They looked like giant dragon flies with four wings. Each wing had a powerful engine near the tip. The engines pivoted down as they landed.

One larger man got out of the first rip-wing, followed by other officers. He wore a jet grey uniform over his large heavy body. His thick round glasses sunk into his puffy round face. The wet grass squished below his boots as he walked up to the house.

"Is this everyone?" he asked an officer who was standing over the prisoners.

"Yes, Inspector Zoddoz."

He walked around the group of prisoners, slowly examining each face. "Are you sure?"

"Yes, sir." replied the officer, "We've searched the entire house."

He stopped at one of the prisoners and squatted down. "And who are you?"

"I am Doctor Bushbeck." said the man.

Mr. Zoddoz squinted his eyes. "If you're a doctor, where's your patient?"

"He's dead."

"And who would that person be?" said Mr. Zoddoz.

"Professor Geoffrey Addha. He was quite ill. His body has been removed from the premises."

"Then what are you all still doing in his house, hmm?"

"Well, he only died yesterday. We've only begun moving out."

"I see." said Mr. Zoddoz, as he got up. "Then, I'm sure you must know the whereabouts of his son?"

"And who would that person be?" said the doctor.

But, with a flick of the wrist he slapped the doctor, knocking him over. There was no cry of pain. The doctor got himself sitting upright again and said nothing more.

"Take them all away." said Mr. Zoddoz. "It's clear that we'll get no help from them, but I want them all detained anyway, and interrogated to the maximum extent." He turned to another group of officers, "I want a full sweep of the house again. And send some officers to search that town nearby, starting with the local train station, and check the nearest network hub for surveillance records."

Inside the injured house, shards of broken glass crunched below his boots as he looked around in the house. Soldiers were breaking down closets and ripping up floorboards. Mr. Zoddoz walked slowly through the sitting room.

There was a hospital bed stripped bare in the middle of the room, and a stain on the floor next to it. He moved on a little and admired some of the glass display cases with their ancient metal suits of armour. He came to one case with its door left open slightly. He looked up at the suit of armour inside behind the glass. With one finger he pulled the door open wide.

His eyes focused on the empty space between the ancient face mask and the decorative outer shell that would've covered a helmet. But there was no helmet, only a space. – A very *clean* space. He tilted his head to one side and smiled. "Ah, yes... so... is *this* where you've been hiding it?" he said under his breath, "– you and the 'professor'? And you think you can keep it from me, do you?"

An officer came in. "Excuse me, sir. We've found surveillance of someone matching Mr. Addha's description boarding a train, late last night. We're still determining where he's gone, though."

"Stop at nothing to find him." said Mr. Zoddoz, pointing, "You must not let him get off this planet." Then Mr. Zoddoz stepped out onto the porch and watched as two of the three rip-wings took off with an electrifying roar, carrying away most of the soldiers and their prisoners. "Well, Mr. Addha," he said under his breath, "so shall begin the hunt..."

~ ~ ~

Elsewhere, far away, far down an endless stretch of tracks, the electric humming sound increased in pitch for a few seconds, then decreased, then faded out as the darkness of a long tunnel transitioned to the gleaming light of a train station.

Mr. Addha awoke from his sleep as the train doors opened. The noise of thousands of people on the platforms, walking this way and that, flooded into his ears. He had arrived at the busy Empire-Central station.

He got himself together, put on his brown leather jacket, grabbed his small suitcase, extended its handle, and pulled it along on its little wheels behind him. He tried to keep his eyes open as he adjusted to the bright light. He stepped off the train with his small, wheeled suitcase onto the platform where several other trains were stopped, and he followed a crowd over to an escalator and upstairs to the star port level – elegant, spacious and red carpeted.

He gazed upward. The huge gracefully arched glass ceiling

welcomed travellers with the spectacle of a hazy morning sky full of shiny star liners, big and small, new and old, coming and going overhead with roaring engines and flashing lights. And looking around the bustling port he spotted a panel.

=ALL FLIGHTS TO AERII=

And he started walking out across the spacious red carpeted floor, pulling with him that small, wheeled suitcase. And as he walked he joined himself to the great mass of people coming and going, merging and converging, each one making their way to the next part of their own journey.

To him, for a moment, the jungle of boarding gates and hallways, and the vast canopy of glass seemed to coalesce into something like a symphony of organized chaos, with all the people and relentless noise and commotion of the vast star port. It was a feeling both familiar and new. And as he pulled that small, wheeled suitcase, he disappeared into the great mass of people.

≈≈≈

And elsewhere, a little later, on the busy street outside a grand centroid, a young sentry officer got off his roller-cycle, removed his visor and looked up at a large sign with grey metal letters.

=CENTROID ELEVEN=

A thick metal and glass door opened with a startling whoosh of air. His steps echoed throughout the spacious lobby as he looked up at the lofty ceiling.

Two polished metal doors lit up cool-white, and silently, slid open. He stepped off the elevator and found his way to one particular office on an upper floor. He entered without knocking, stopped and stood there without speaking, and glanced around the office. Everyone looked up from their desks. Mr. Salter, looking concerned, got up from his desk and approached the officer. But the officer focused on two empty office rooms and read the names on each doorway.

One read: Chief Inspector Addha, and the other: Senior Inspector Gruffly. Finally, he turned to Mr. Salter and without saying a word, handed him a small square envelope marked: *Gruffly.*

As the officer left, Mr. Salter held the envelope up to the light of the window. There was the shape of a small disk inside.

≈≈≈

And yet elsewhere, and later still, an older man in a raincoat entered a bright glass and stone building, near the harbour. There was a round desk with a few men and women in white uniforms. A woman greeted him. He showed his badge and asked a question. She consulted a light leaf in her hand and led him down a hall with polished floors and white walls.

They entered a large room divided into several areas with white curtains. In each area there was a medical bed. She led him to one bed in particular, with a man sleeping on it, then she walked away, leaving him there.

He looked down at the man – about 35 years of age – sleeping, recovering from burns he had suffered from charge pistol shots. It was the man that Mr. Gruffly had shot the day before, at the house of Lord Sage, when he rescued Mr. Addha. A light leaf chart hung on the wall beside his bed. He could see all of the read-outs displayed on the chart. He looked around to see if anyone was watching him, then picked up the chart. His eyes skipped up to the top, over the graphs and numbers, up to the first few lines, with the patient's name and personal information. The young man on the hospital bed slowly opened his grey eyes and looked at him. – It was David Sage.

To be continued...

DREAMS OF GLASS